We Are
All We Have

ALSO BY MARINA BUDHOS

The Long Ride
Watched

We Are All We Have

MARINA BUDHOS

WENDY
LAMB
BOOKS

Text copyright © 2022 by Marina Budhos
Jacket art copyright © 2022 by Samya Arif

All rights reserved. Published in the United States by Wendy Lamb Books, an imprint of Random House Children's Books, a division of Penguin Random House LLC, New York.

Wendy Lamb Books and the colophon are trademarks of Penguin Random House LLC.

Permissions for ghazals appear on pages 239–241.
Permission for the quote on page vii courtesy of the Southern Poverty Law Center (SPLC).

Visit us on the Web! GetUnderlined.com

Educators and librarians, for a variety of teaching tools, visit us at RHTeachersLibrarians.com

Library of Congress Cataloging-in-Publication Data is available upon request.
ISBN 978-0-593-12020-0 (hardcover) — ISBN 978-0-593-12021-7 (lib. bdg.) —
ISBN 978-0-593-12022-4 (ebook)

The text of this book is set in 11.5-point Adobe Garamond Pro.
Interior design by Michelle Crowe

Printed in the United States of America
10 9 8 7 6 5 4 3 2 1
First Edition

To those seeking safety—may their stories be heard.

On May 7, 2018, the US Department of Justice (DOJ) announced it had implemented a "zero tolerance" policy, dictating that all migrants who cross the border without permission, including those seeking asylum, be referred to the DOJ for prosecution. Undocumented asylum seekers were imprisoned, and any accompanying children under the age of eighteen were handed over to the US Department of Health and Human Services (HHS), which shipped them miles away from their parents and scattered them among one hundred Office of Refugee Resettlement (ORR) shelters and other care arrangements across the country. Hundreds of these children, including infants and toddlers, were under the age of five.

—**Southern Poverty Law Center (SPLC)**

Their faces assumed the awful craftiness of children listening for sounds from the grown-up world.

—**J. M. Barrie,** *Peter Pan*

I

Brooklyn, New York

2019

Chapter One

They're coming.

It takes a second for the words to drip into the thick soup of my sleep.

They're here.

The words make ripples in my half dreams. A lamp switches on and a bright band of light stings my lids. "Rania! They're *here.*"

I wrench up from the quilt, my heart quivering. "Who?"

"Just come." Ammi nods to the other bed, where my little brother, Kamal, is sleeping. "Don't wake him."

"Of course," I grumble. I punch my pillow and force myself to get up. Kamal is protected. *He's sensitive. Don't let him hear.* With me, her voice is flat, practical.

I follow her out of the bedroom; she's still in her jacket from work—a black windbreaker that makes a rubbing noise as she walks. The keys are still in the open door. She hasn't even pulled out her sofa bed.

Several people are crowded outside our apartment. The fizzing, garbled sound of a walkie-talkie from the hall cuts through our living room. My heart speeds up. They're in black quilted vests with POLICE on the back.

No. Not us.

A woman turns to me, the one with the walkie-talkie. "Hold," she says, and clicks off. "And this is?"

"My daughter."

"Any other children in the apartment?"

"My son."

"And your daughter is how old?"

A hesitation. "Eighteen."

"Ammi—" I start, but she flashes me a cool, forbidding look.

That's a lie! I want to yell. I'm not eighteen for seven months— December. I'm tall, very tall, taking after my dad, so most people think I'm older than I am. I get away with a lot: the teachers who don't say a word when I come to pick up my little brother; the kids who hit on me to buy them beer at the liquor store. Me and Ammi both stretch the truth when we have to.

The woman looks up at me. "We'll have to see some ID, then."

Ammi gives her one of her charming smiles. "Can you wait just a moment?" She takes my arm and draws me into the foyer.

"Ammi!" I whisper. "My ID says I'm seventeen! Why did you—"

"Hush." She sets her hands on my shoulders. Ammi is so short, she has to lift her chin to meet my gaze, but she can still terrify me with one firm look. "No time for panic or baby stuff."

"I'm not a baby!"

Her eyes dart in a dozen directions. "There's a plan—"

"What plan?" I yank up my sweatpants, worrying the string.

"I tried to call Maria Auntie but she's not home. She's on a shift."

"Why did you say I was eighteen?"

"Rania!" She shakes me lightly. "You're minors. You can't be left on your own."

On our own? My eyes swing around the foyer. Wait. Panic starts up in my chest. Ammi can't go.

She's fumbling inside a table drawer, taking out an envelope. Ammi once showed me the paper inside, explaining, "If anything happens, this is what you need. It's a standby guardianship form. Maria Auntie will take care of you."

Maria Auntie lives down the hall and is our surrogate aunt since we don't have any family in this country. She brings us foil dishes of arepas and tamales and we keep our extra keys with her. Maria Auntie is a lot like Ammi—she's got hustles and side hustles to keep her family going.

"Everything okay over there?" the officer calls over to us.

Ammi pulls me back to the doorway. "My mistake. My daughter is eighteen in a few months."

The woman gives us a skeptical look. "So you've appointed a standby guardian?"

"Yes, yes." She thrusts the folded paper at the officer, who reads it.

"And where is Maria Alvarez?"

My mother's voice fades. "Working."

The woman squints at the form. "And who is this—Lucia Alvarez?"

"Lucia!" my mother says brightly. "Yes, yes! She is home. Maria's daughter."

Oh great, I think. Lucia. The biggest mess-up around. She dropped out of LaGuardia College and got in trouble with some creepy boyfriend.

The officer goes down the hall and presses, hard, on Maria Auntie's buzzer. A few other doors in the hall crack open, some still with the chain attached, worried faces peering out. I feel a humiliating burn around my ears. We have seen this before. Men and women in these same jackets swarming up the stairs. Calling through the door. Crying and pleading and then our neighbors were gone.

"Who is it?"

Before the officer can speak, Ammi calls out, "It's us! Sadia and Rania!"

The door swings open. Lucia's makeup is smeary, one side of her curly hair flattened. "Yeah?"

When the officer explains the situation, she rolls her eyes, as if to say, *You guys are always a pain.* I've heard her complain to Maria Auntie that they shouldn't get involved with other people's problems.

There's a footfall behind me. Turning, I see Kamal in his rumpled pajamas, rubbing his eyes. "Ammi?" he mumbles.

My mother looks crushed. Everything she does is to never let Kamal know this could happen. Me, I'm always supposed to go along with her, even if it makes no sense.

"Take him back in," the walkie-talkie woman says to Ammi, firm.

"May I say goodbye?"

The woman sighs. "This isn't a good idea."

My whole body clenches. Every part of me wants to scream: *Then don't take my mother.*

Ammi kneels down. She's in slacks and a crisp shirt, as if

4

for an office, even though she's been driving all night for Uber. Kamal stretches his thin arms around her neck and nestles in her hair. She's murmuring to him calmly. I'm furious—and scared. Then Ammi wipes her eyes.

"Ma'am?"

"Just a minute."

"Ma'am, don't make this harder."

She stands. She puts something in my palm—cool and bumpy—it's her keys, to the car, to everything else. She draws me close. I smell sandalwood and a trace of coconut oil in her hair, the stuff that I use for my unruly waves. My mother is so young, it's as if we're sisters, not mother and daughter. "You can drive," she whispers. "Remember that."

True. Ammi made sure I took driver's ed, even though I use buses and the subway everywhere. She never lets me drive the car. But she's always ready to flee. We keep a suitcase packed with a set of overnight clothes and toothbrushes in the bottom of our closet; we never buy too much for the apartment—one wok, one tawa pan, silverware for four, so we always have to wash our forks and knives after eating. The story of our life, for so long.

But this time, it's not the three of us, packed up, sprung and ready to go. Just her. I call out, "Wait! It's a mistake!"

Ammi pulls back. Her face has gone hard. "Not now, Rania."

I whimper.

"In the morning, call Lidia. She knows what to do." That's our lawyer.

My mother and I stare at each other. A staticky voice comes

through the walkie-talkie. "We need you down here. Another group. A van."

"Roger that," the woman says. "I've got some collateral here too."

Collateral.

Ammi.

The woman gestures to Lucia, who grudgingly comes and stands by our door. "You're over eighteen?"

Lucia looks defiant. "Just turned the big twenty."

"Can I see ID?"

Here Lucia's bravado falters. She's undocumented. The whole family is. She fishes out an ID, the woman scribbles down the information, then gives it back. "Okay, you'll need to stay with them. We'll send someone to make sure your mother is serving as standby."

The officer gently takes my mother's elbow and guides her past half-opened doors and frightened faces. Kamal flings his arms around me, presses his head into my stomach.

Lucia nervously picks at her fingers. Behind her toughness, she's scared. Just like us. She puts her hand on Kamal's back. "Thanks," I whisper.

And then we are watching, stunned, as Ammi disappears down the stairwell, swallowed up in a mound of heads and shoulders. It's only after she leaves that it sinks in.

This was a raid. An ICE raid.

I wrench Kamal into our apartment, slam the door, and push down a sob. No. I can't break down in front of Kamal. Back in our bedroom, I nudge him into bed. Even though he's trembling and confused, he slides his bare feet under the blanket and turns his back to me. I rush to the window. Down below, several ICE agents mill in the hot glare of lights. One puts a palm on Ammi's head, steering her toward the back of the van. She glances up at me, to our window. I see her mouth move.

Run, I'm sure she's saying. *Run.*

Chapter Two

Two months ago I was running around for fun.

It was early April, one of those hot days where sweat pricks the back of your neck the minute you step outside. I had just dropped off Kamal at school and was heading over to the subway to meet my best friend, Fatima. This was our routine every day since we met at the beginning of ninth grade in gym class. On that day, I was groaning and cursing my thick hair falling in my face when a girl handed me a gold-braided tie, saying, "Take it. I've made fifty more." She had the same wild waves as me, but she looked way more chic with her gray-green eyes, her drab uniform shorts rolled into neat cuffs. I snapped the band into place and felt sleek and cool.

Now, by spring of senior year, it's like there's a wind under our sneakers. Fatima and I glide and slide through the Brooklyn streets—my neighborhood, Sunset Park; hers in Bay Ridge. Our shoulders loosened back, not bowed with textbooks. All that counted is behind us. Sure, we've got our Regents exams but I'm not too worried. We're in the fourth quarter, our grades stacking up fine. I've got my admission to Hunter College in Manhattan; after lots of family drama, Fatima's going to Brooklyn College.

On that day we were wearing matching FREEDOM T-shirts that Fatima designed, showing a silhouette of two girls before a sunset. Our little reward to ourselves for four years of manic work and pushing for grades, while taking care of our siblings and re-membering to pull the meat out of the freezer for dinner—so what if we declared ourselves free a little early? We deserve it.

Self-care, Fatima calls it. She's always posting pics on Insta-gram on how to give yourself a spa day or light scented candles to soothe your spirit. Blissful pictures of windows looking out on the Mediterranean Sea or of us lounging in Sunset Park, show-ing off our pedis. Fatima's something fierce about fashion and self-love. I'm sure it's because of her mother, who got married at sixteen. Mrs. Elawady is always in the same long housedress, day in, day out, too busy with taking care of Fatima and her three brothers. Fatima gets furious at her mother for letting her roots grow out; now and then she drags her into the bathroom, packs her hair with her grandmother's recipe of henna and yogurt. I think Mrs. Elawady likes it, actually. "My daughter, the bossy general. I always obey."

That's the biggest thing we have in common: our moms. Young-old, we say. We'll never be like them. We'll fly fast before life tugs us by the ankles. Isn't that the whole reason they came to America? Fatima's mother thought she was going to go to uni-versity in Cairo to be a nurse, until her parents told her about a great match: a young man who already owned a business in the US. After many cups of mint tea, talking about the two young people, the matter was settled between the families. "No way that's how my life's decided!" Fatima often declares.

Now, on this warm spring morning, I found Fatima waiting

by the subway entrance. She had on a denim jacket to hide how tight her T-shirt pulled across her chest. I'm sure her mom wasn't too thrilled about that. "I got the afternoon off," she told me.

"Me too. Kamal is going to a friend's place."

"Wanna go downtown after school?"

"Oh yeah."

"Freedom!" We laughed, bumped fists. She hooked her arm through mine, and we raced onto the platform, ignoring the people who frowned at us. We grabbed a couple of seats while the train rumbled underground for a few stops and then suddenly we were up, aboveground, sunlight shooting through the glass. We stared out at the blinding morning light, slashing across the Brooklyn rooftops. Everyone else was lost in their phones or staring down at their shoes. They didn't even notice the view! That's what me and Fatima wanted: to live full on, taking in everything.

Our FREEDOM T-shirts came from when we were studying the Beats with Mr. D junior year and reading Jack Kerouac's *On the Road*. I complained that the main characters are just a bunch of sexist white dudes who get to do whatever they want, and all the women are called girls and get dumped. "Go ahead, rewrite it," he told us.

So I did. We performed our feminist version for Mr. D's Beat Café Night. Brooklyn Ra-Ra and Fa-Fa, we called ourselves. We sat on folding chairs, in black felt berets, on our own wild road trip to find America. At the end I got up and gave my last riff:

The road is a licorice whip sliding down my throat
red-bean buns in Sunset Park, watching the sky blush pink.
West, go West, the Beats told us.

What if the road isn't yours because the guys got there first?
Maybe the road is your head bristling with possibilities,
The America of me
not the Mexican girl left behind in California,
the jazz players of Denver.
We want America too but our mothers say:
Be careful. Watch out. Curb your mouth. Bring in the laundry.
How do you find America when you've got dinner to make?
When you can't kiss that boy under a Red Hook moon?
I am not my mother I am me
How do I find the America that is me?

We got a lot of cheers, some howling, kids punching the air.
Mr. D. submitted that and some of my other writing to a contest.
I won a scholarship for "literary promise," which will help pay for
Hunter College. Meanwhile, Fatima fought with her parents to
go to FIT, the Fashion Institute of Technology, but her father put
his foot down and said she was going to Brooklyn College, since
it's closer to home, and she'll major in something more practical. Still we made promises to meet up in Prospect Park or rove
around the city as much as we could.

Our version of free.

— — —

We stopped at the corner bodega, dunked our hands in the cooler
of chilled water, and grabbed a couple of bottles, ice thudding inside. I walked with a bottle pressed against my neck and crossed
the street to the park to watch the cute boys on the basketball

court. "Fa-tee-ma!" this guy Jamal called, with his loose, easy smile. "When you hangin' with me?"

"Never!" she called back.

Ammi always says to me, "Wait for the true one, Rania. Protect your heart." No worries there. I wouldn't waste my time on these losers anyway. My eyes are locked on next year and beyond.

The bell rang and we were part of the bumpy rush to pour into the huge building, banging up to the third floor so we weren't late. My breaths were hot and sharp in my lungs by the time I got to Ms. Ricardo's English class. Not that I worried: she'd gone light on me ever since I got the scholarship. Just as I was sitting down, my phone buzzed: a text from my mother.

Kamal's taken care of?

I shoved the phone to my pocket but it vibrated. *Rania? U there?*

In class. I told you. Yes.

Where again?

His friend. Derek.

Sorry. Home late tonight.

Totally annoying. We just went over the arrangements an hour ago! Ammi said she had to visit immigration in the afternoon. A routine check: she does it every year while our asylum application makes its way through the system. Each time she goes I feel a spike of fear. Especially these days, with what we see on the news. The Muslim ban. No more asylum seekers allowed. But this morning Ammi insisted it was nothing, just the usual rubber stamp. I watched her slide off her bangle. "Why are you doing that?" I asked. She gave me a blank smile. "It's been rubbing me lately." As if to prove it, she kneaded her wrist. That didn't make sense. The bangle came from my father, a long time ago, when they married. I listened to it drop, clinking, into a bowl.

— — —

After school, I spotted Fatima squatting by a wall and taking a picture where someone had graffitied BROOKLYN IS LOVE in bright fuzzy letters. She tucked her phone in her pocket. "Another idea for a T-shirt. I can sell it on Etsy."

Fatima's always coming up with creative schemes like this: she stays up late sewing sequins onto shirt collars, or cuts up her mother's old housedresses to make patchwork turbans. Last year she made all of ninety-seven dollars, but she's still sure that this will be her life.

"You'll major in accounting," her dad told her. After I don't know how many fights and tears and her texting me at all hours of the night, she agreed, telling me that at least with an accounting degree, no one will cheat her when she opens her own clothing line. Fatima's not one to back down easily. "You're so lucky," she says. "Your mom is a warrior. She wants you to be a writer. Or whatever you want."

It's not that simple.

What I really feel: my mom wants to be me.

Ever since I could remember, I've felt my mother's wistful breaths on my neck. Fingering my stuff. Telling me about how she was a good writer in school too, the ghazals she used to scribble, the plays she acted in. Sometimes I'd come home and find Ammi on my bed, one of my schoolbooks opened on the pillow. She'd get up, groggy, strands of moist curly hair pressed against her cheek. Sadness and fury boiled up inside me. *My* bed, the quilt dented with her body. *My* book, pages folded on the corners. She was always there, her lingering scent of coconut oil and detergent, smothering my thoughts.

And then I'd feel badly. Ammi brought me here, on her own, and never complains. She's tiny, just over five feet, and moves down the street like a boxer, using her shoulders to press past a crowd. She likes to shop on Eighth Avenue, Chinatown, where she says the long beans are the best, and she bargains down the fishmongers, who stand poised in their rubber aprons, paper bags open, or elbows into the cluster of Chinese women buying packages of pajamas spread on the pavement. She's blunt and unsentimental. When I ask her about our family, her eyes flash, and she says, "You want to know how the men treat their wives and daughters? No, I don't think so." And that was the end of that.

Fatima and I crossed the street, headed toward the subway. "My parents asked me how I'd feel about delaying college a year."

I stopped. "No way! You can't do that!"

"I think my dad's trying to set up a match. He'd rather have me married so I can cut out the whole dating-in-college thing."

"No! Don't listen to him!" I pushed the hurt out of my voice. "What about our plans next year? Hanging out? Your fashion line?"

She sent her voice into a low, manly roll. " 'Fatima, marriage isn't some kind of shopping spree. You can't return what you bought the next day!' "

"He did not say that."

"Totally."

"What does your mom say? Didn't she always tell you that she wouldn't let the same happen to you?"

Fatima shrugged. "What my dad says goes in our house. You know that."

I don't hate many people. But I hate Mr. Elawady. He's old-school, big-time. I hate how he pushes into the house stomach first, and suddenly everyone's shouting. I hate how he brushes aside anything Fatima says and he has to sit at the head of the table lecturing and never listening. He makes my head ache. But most of all I hate how he makes me feel: ashamed. A few years ago Ammi wanted to take us on a day trip in her new car to Asbury Park on the Jersey Shore. But Fatima's father put his foot down. Her mom doesn't even drive. If she needs to run an errand, either her brother or one of the drivers from Mr. Elawady's limousine business takes her. "If Rania's mother had a husband, he would not allow such a thing," he told Fatima.

Not my abu, I thought. My father was a free spirit.

We reached a corner and I pressed the button at the crosswalk. "I think he's just messing around," I told her "Just so *you* won't mess around."

"It's so unfair." Fatima punched angrily at the button too. "He lets Abdul do anything. Date anyone! He gets a speeding ticket, my dad slaps him on the back and laughs, says, I was a terror like you too!"

"Just don't do anything stupid, Fa-Fa."

The light switched; we walked in grumpy silence toward the subway. These were our favorite kinds of afternoons, so rare, when we tried to squeeze in every drop of time. Usually I was on Kamal duty, or doing the grocery shopping, dragging Ammi's cart, and Fatima had to help her mother or her father's business, where he yelled at the half cousins who sauntered in and wanted

Fatima to put in a good word for them. Our lives: a bunch of negotiations for freedom. "There's no such thing as freedom," her mother once said to us. "You girls need to get that out of your heads right now. Then you will be much happier."

I like Mrs. Elawady. She has this rough rasp in her voice, like a cold engine turning over, since she secretly smokes. Her hair is always frizzed, and she's usually smacking a big hand in the air toward one of Fatima's little brothers. But she's relaxed, comfortable with herself. Behind the scenes she's always working on her husband, trying to make him go easier on Fatima. Maybe with this marriage thing, she's just indulging him so Fatima can get what she wants.

After a few stops we emerged into downtown Brooklyn, where we wandered along Fulton Street Mall, checking out tops. Later we crossed into Fort Greene, which was lined with fancy brownstones and expensive little restaurants.

When we stopped in at a bookstore, I got an idea. I walked right up to the cashier and asked if they were hiring. She called the manager, Amirah. When I saw her walking toward me—a tall, slender woman wearing a red-and-black-printed headscarf—I felt a small pulse of excitement. I'd do anything to work for someone so cool and beautiful.

After I filled out the application and she went over it, she asked, "So you like literature?"

"Kind of runs in the family. My mom wanted to be an English professor."

"What about you?"

I felt my skin prickle. Amirah's question made me nervous, as if there were a spotlight trained on me. I was so used to talking about myself in relation to Ammi, never just me. "Probably going to be an English major. Totally impractical."

"I majored in Russian," she said and we laughed.

We talked some more about authors and poetry, and at the end, she said, "I'm definitely going to be hiring at the end of the summer. A lot of the college kids who work for us in the summer will be going back. You say you're going where?"

"Hunter."

"Great. You're local." She stood, and shook my hand. "It all looks good. I'll be in touch about training." She added, "I warn you. A lot of it is really boring. Unboxing books. Inventory."

"I'm in."

After she went back to her office, I bought myself a new lilac-colored notebook. I couldn't wait to crack it open, smooth down the pages, put my name inside.

When I rejoined Fatima, she was so excited she declared I needed to buy myself something more. A few blocks down a Jamaican dude in aviator sunglasses was blasting reggae from an old boom box. Vintage clothes were spread out on a blanket on the pavement and hanging from a fence. Fatima lit up, touching an orange vinyl jacket with brass buttons, a daisy-print dress, and a pair of maroon corduroy bell-bottoms. She snatched up an old army jacket, its epaulets embroidered purple, and held it up to me.

"Try it."

I slipped it on, swept my hair up over the collar, and turned to the narrow mirror. "Beautiful girl!" the guy said.

I looked at the epaulets that made my shoulders straight and firm, the frayed cuff, and the heavy buttons, and it instantly felt like mine. I was toughened, protected. Everything that lay ahead—graduation, summer, maybe my first real job—and then onward into the fall, where I could lace up my favorite black boots, shrug on this jacket, put my new notebook into my bag, and take the subway into Manhattan, to college, a new life. This jacket smelled and felt like my future.

"How much?" I asked.

His sunglasses glinted. "Twenty-five, for you."

I shook my head, started pulling it off.

"Twenty!"

I dipped the hanger into the sleeve and hooked it back onto the fence.

"Fifteen." He sounded desperate.

I swiveled, giving him a sweet, slow smile. "Deal."

I was ready. For all of it.

— — —

It was late by the time I got home. Kamal was already there, sitting cross-legged on the rug, watching TV. Maria Auntie had just picked him up from Derek's since she was nearby, and then she left to walk dogs and close up a nearby laundromat. Maria Auntie may juggle a lot of jobs—I can't keep track—but she always has time for us. Ammi texted to say she was on her way home too. I ducked into the bedroom to do my homework. When my stomach started to growl, I looked up. It was over an hour since her text—so not like her. To hold us over, I scrambled eggs with chili peppers and tomatoes that Kamal and I folded into naan. We were just finishing up when Ammi barged into the apartment.

"Ammi, we were starving—" I stopped. Her hair was a tumbled mess, sprung loose from its band; kohl smeared, her eyes two worried holes. Her clothes were creased and wrinkled. She set down a white bag of takeout, spotted with grease.

"So sorry, beta." She kissed the top of Kamal's head. "I got delayed."

"But where—"

She brushed past me toward the bathroom. "There are kebabs. Rice, the way you like it. I'm going to take a shower."

And then she slammed the door. I heard needles of water tinging on the tub, and a low warbling sound. Crying. I stared at the bag, my stomach twisting, anxious. The kebabs were cold, as if they'd been sitting around a long time. We ate in silence and still Ammi hadn't come out. Great. That meant more chores for me—cleaning up, helping Kamal get ready for bed. I was about to tell her about my bookstore job, then stuffed it back down. I knew what she'd say: What about your responsibilities at home? Or worse, she'd show up and start chatting up Amirah about all the books she knew.

I fell asleep reading, and a few hours later, I startled awake. My novel had slid to the floor. Someone had switched off my lamp. A seam of light leaked under my door. Creeping out of bed, I found Ammi sitting at the dining room table, staring at the laptop screen. A cone of bluish light revealed all the grooves of her face.

Noticing me, she snapped the laptop shut, pushed some

papers into an accordion file, and offered a bright, blank look. "Oh, darling, can't sleep?"

"You okay?" I shuffled closer.

She took my hand, pressed it against her cheek. I was surprised at its warmth—the computer light made her skin look coated in ice, forbidding.

"Of course," she whispered.

But I could hear it—the tiniest wrinkle in her voice.

The sound of worry.

Chapter Three

"She was refused her stay," Lidia, our lawyer, states, leaning forward on her desk. It's the morning after the ICE raid, and I'm in Lidia's office. "Your mom's last visit—two months ago—they told her to start preparing to leave." She sighs. "It was a courtesy, actually. Even giving her this much time. The officers know her by now. They like her."

"You've got to stop it! Call them up! Tell them it's a mistake!" I pace the small room and keep bumping into the coffee table stacked high with folders.

"Calm down, Rania. Please."

"But I'm supposed to graduate in three weeks! Why now?"

"Rania! You're making me dizzy."

I drop down in a chair, my backpack mounded on my lap. I'd barely slept. Once the sun pushed through our blinds, I jumped out of bed, my mouth tasting as if it were filled with ash. Numb, I managed to drag Kamal to school, then text Fatima, who skipped our first class to meet at our favorite diner, so I could tell her that they'd taken Ammi away. We sat in the booth sipping coffee, raw, bewildered.

Now I ask Lidia, "They told her this when she did her last check-in?"

"Yes. You've had a removal order hanging over you for years. That's what we've been fighting."

So that's why Ammi was late and strange that day. Ammi had always told me that even though we were denied asylum the first time, and again during our merits hearing, our appeal was going well. The board would surely understand. Look at who she was! The widow of a brave journalist. An impeccable background. A university degree. English-speaking. Posh English, even! "We're the kind of immigrant they want." *Snap-shut,* she'd sing, after a meeting with Lidia. "Just a few technicalities."

When I explain this to Lidia, she looks at me sadly. "She told you that?"

I nod.

"And you believed her?"

That ash taste in my mouth again. "Why wouldn't I believe my mother?"

Lidia takes a long draw from her mug with a silver bombilla, a straw, and sets it down. I've always liked Lidia, with her head of black curly hair, same as Ammi and me. She speaks in a quick, mash-up accent—Spanish and Southern—since she's from Argentina, but she moved to Tennessee with her family as a teenager. "You should have seen me next to all the debutantes!" she laughs. "I didn't fit in one bit." The drink is mate, she'd once told me, which fuels her through hectic days.

I ask, "She was lying to me?"

"Not exactly lying. Just minimizing."

There's a heat growing around my cheeks, tightening my scalp. "What do you mean?"

"There have always been problems with her case. Getting testimony from others that she truly had to flee—"

"That's bs! I remember! We packed really fast!"

Lidia moves closer, soothing. "Darling, I know. But your mother. She has her own ideas . . ."

No kidding. Ammi always has to do things her way. When I was younger, she'd show up to parent-teacher conferences, all decked out with blue eye shadow and dangling silver earrings, and insist that I be given harder books to read, extra math homework. She'd make sure the teacher knew that she'd almost finished her MPhil. After, she'd complain that the teacher seemed no more educated than a cashier, and she could do a better job teaching that class. I'd shrink inside. Why did a conference about me have to be about her? Her lousy jobs, driving an Uber, has not smoothed down her pride, not one bit.

"But why now?"

"A few weeks ago we found out her stay had been denied. I don't think she was expecting that."

The appeal: It's hung over us for a few years, ever since she was denied asylum in the first go-round. Those fat folders my mother keeps locked in a closet and pulls out now and then, spreading them out on the dining table. Every time I'd ask her about it, she'd give me a sad smile and say, "I worry about the past. And you the future. That's your job."

Lidia continues, "Now this raid. They weren't even looking for her. But she was just coming home—"

"They weren't?" I feel faint. *Collateral.* That's what they said over the walkie-talkie. Ammi was an extra prize. "Can't you just tell them that she wasn't supposed to be taken?"

Lidia nods, tired. "We have to go before a judge. Explain that she's on appeal."

"How long will that take?" I ask. "And what about me? And Kamal?"

"You're part of your mother's asylum case. We do have a separate juvenile-immigrant-status file for you too."

"So let's use that!"

"Rania, slow down. We're waiting on that as well. Let's start where we are. The situation with DACA for undocumented children like you is even worse. I'm sure you've heard the news—"

She's interrupted by a knock on the door and Lidia's assistant, Sylvie, pops her head in. Behind her, phones ring, people talk. It was more crowded than usual when I picked my way through Lidia's office. "I have Mr. Chan on the line," Sylvie says. "He says they didn't accept the job verification he uploaded and the deadline is today—"

Lidia sighs and turns back to me. "I'm so sorry. I'm going to have to take this. I'm helping out one of our partners who usually takes these cases."

"Wait, my mother!" I cry. Only my mother matters. Her case. Ours. Me.

"Just tell him I'll call back in five," Lidia says to her assistant.

"But the deadline—" Sylvie says.

Lidia waves her hand. Once the door shuts, it's as if the room were suddenly cast in cold shadow. "They never used to bother with cases like your mother's. She checked in, year in, year out.

It was routine. But the situation is volatile now. Every day it's another rule, another policy change." She shakes her head. "Zero tolerance, they call it. The raids are out of control. I think they're trying to fill some kind of quota. To show they're tough on immigration. Or that call I just got. A simple H1B renewal. Now they make my clients jump through hoops to prove they aren't taking a job from an American."

I don't care about policies or words like *zero tolerance*. I just want to see my mother—my stubborn, proud, impossible mother. I want to fight with her, put my arms around her, feel her scraggly curls against my throat. I want her to bustle into our bedroom and fling open the curtains, chide Kamal while gently slapping his bare soles. I want it all—the mess of combs and lotions and soaps she leaves in the bathroom, her unmade bed in the living room, her bossy instructions before she heads off for an Uber shift, or all her other jobs—cat sitting, plant watering, dropping off the dry cleaning for the old lady on the first floor. I want my summer, my life back. I'm supposed to give that up? And why does Lidia call it *her* application? It's my life. My future. How much am I supposed to give up?

"Can I see her?" My voice cracks.

"That's what I'm working on. They have her in a facility in Pennsylvania."

"Pennsylvania!" I can barely breathe.

"I can't say whether that's better or worse. My clients who go to Elizabeth, New Jersey, right next to Newark Airport, are put on a plane home."

Home? Ammi often says, *I would sooner die than step back into that country that took your father. That family that has forsaken me.*

Her eyes are so angry, I know not to ask more. But I wonder: Pakistan was my abu, the three of us happy, laughing over supper at night. Or skipping to school in my light blue shalwar kameez and racing the chowkidar's son across the courtyard. It wasn't all terrible; it was the first part of my life. But Ammi doesn't want to hear that.

"Look, I have a call in. I've pulled out all the stops. If it works out, is Saturday good?"

I give her a shaky head bob. "Yes."

She gets up, puts her arms around me, and hugs me firmly. Her hair gives off a floral scent. The door swings open again, noise buzzing around us, but she grips me harder, whispering, "I'm so sorry, Rania. So sorry."

— — —

In the elevator, standing in front of me, is a girl my age dressed up. Her collar is tacked in the back with a safety pin, ready to come loose. That pin makes me want to cry. Everything feels so patched together. Maybe she's one of Lidia's clients, on her way to court. I want to ask her: Are you scared too?

Outside, I wobble a few steps on the street and stop. There's a garbage bin in front of me. I swing my leg at it and kick and kick, pain jolting through my boot toe. The ash taste in my mouth surges up. I stagger over to the side and throw up onto a grate. I can feel people bumping past me, but I don't care. I let it all out, head bent, elbows on my knees, until I'm scraped raw.

"Hey! You okay?"

A thin, blond woman hovers near. She looks worried, but also a little grossed out.

"Yeah," I say weakly. "Greasy breakfast."

"I've had bad days too." She pulls out a water bottle from her bag. "Why don't you take it?"

I cradle the cold bottle against my chest, watch her walk off, hiking her bag up on her shoulder. I want to call after her and say, "Please, take me with you. My mom's gone. In a detention center. Pennsylvania."

But the words would make no sense. Nothing makes sense.

— — —

That afternoon Kamal and I are dragging up the stairs, since the elevator is broken, when we're met by the glaring eyes of our next-door neighbor Mrs. Flannery.

"There you are!" She's elderly and rarely goes out, except to push her grocery cart down to Key Food. Sometimes she sits on a folding chair in the front, scowling at the street, complaining at the kids on bikes or the delivery guys who park their scooters. She wears large glasses that give her eyes a cloudy, swollen look. In the beginning, Ammi befriended her, bringing over food or offering to fetch something at the store. I think Ammi had an angle—maybe Mrs. Flannery could get us into a better school, even give her a teaching job. But at some point she soured on us. She would slam her door, or if she heard us in the hall, she'd crack it open and peer with her angry eyes. At least half a dozen times she complained that she heard Kamal's video games through her wall.

"So, that was quite a lot of nonsense the other night!" she declares. She is standing with her cart, which is filled with V8 cans. "What did your mother do?"

I wince. "She didn't do anything. It was a mistake."

"Mistake," she sniffs.

"It was," I say evenly and look her in the eye.

"There were some people looking for you too."

I stiffen. "People?"

"They didn't say who they were. But I *know*."

We'll send someone, the ICE officer said.

I look down at her cart. "Would you like some help, taking that in?"

Mrs. Flannery reels backward, offended. "I am an independent woman!" She swivels around, dragging the cart down the hall. I can hear her fumble for her keys, scrabbling with her bag's zippers, but I don't say anything. Ammi always tells me: Stay polite—she's just an old woman, bitter because her own daughter never visits her.

Back in the apartment the first thing I see is a flat plastic package sitting on the table. My graduation cap and gown that I picked up the other day at school. I hurl it into our bedroom closet, not caring that it's crumpled next to my shoes. Folded on my dresser are my new, swingy pants from Ammi for Eid. Pieces start falling into place: how Ammi didn't want to go to a party, like we usually do—distant friends we rarely see. Instead she made koftas and rice and put out a platter of sweets and dates. Then she sat us down in the living room to give us our presents. "It's better just us!" she exclaimed. But her eyes were shadowed, her hands so pale. This Ramzan she'd done the night shift again and again, saying she was too tired from fasting during the day to celebrate. Now I see all she was holding inside while holding tight to us.

I make supper for Kamal and watch over his homework. The whole time I can hear my mother's voice ringing inside me, like rusty bells: *You never knew what it was to grow up so fast.*

What about me? I want to say back. *This isn't exactly slow going.*

But it was always her story, not mine, that loomed over us. How she'd met Abu at university—she was the same age I am—a spunky girl, daughter of a military man. They'd drink cups of chai at the student canteen and argue all the time. Abu came from the wrong kind of family—poor, Shia, not even from Lahore. She knew her family would never approve. But he was brilliant. He had a tongue like a sword, slaying the dragons of corruption and intolerance. From the time he was a little boy, he knew he was going to be a journalist.

He just didn't know he would disappear as one.

Or that he'd disappear from me too.

Maria Auntie comes over as I finish washing up. She puts her arms around me. "Don't worry. Lidia will take care of everything and get your mother out."

"But you . . . you can be our guardian, right?"

Her eyes seem glassy, focused on the wall behind me. I remember the fights I sometimes heard behind their door: about some brush with the cops Lucia had a few months ago. The money Lucia's boyfriend borrowed. And Lucia flinging back that her mom was always busy with everyone else's business.

Maria Auntie taps the foil and points to a bag of groceries

that she's brought. "Lucia will bring some soup tomorrow." She peers at me. "Kamal okay?"

I blink back tears. She didn't answer my question. "He's scared, but he doesn't know what's going on."

"Better that way."

Is it? I want to say. All these years I didn't know the truth about my mother's asylum application. Now Maria Auntie adds, "I'll speak to your lawyer. Everything will work out."

After she leaves, I check my phone and see Fatima texted.

Ra Ra u there? U OK?

Fine.

What did Lidia say?

Complicated.

Talk?

Not now.

What r u gonna do???

Dunno. I send her a chain of sad emojis and then just turn off the phone. What hurts more: that they want us to leave? Or that my mother lied to me?

All this time.

— — —

I fall asleep on the sofa, then wake to a loud noise, my heart banging in my ribs. Just a door slamming down the hall. The TV is on mute, the picture a streaky blur. We used to watch the news all the time after the election. We were terrified: First the Muslim ban, when suddenly anyone from a Muslim country couldn't travel here. Ammi and I would stay up, munching on bowls of chaat, unable to pry ourselves away from the terrible images: the crowds at the airport, the bobbing signs. Me and Fatima snuck out to go to protests, our voices hoarse from shouting. The family down the hall, from Yemen, would troop into the elevator, gray-faced; they told us they weren't able to go back for the funeral of the wife's mother. Months later, the news shifted to the border: tired families lined up; babies hiked to hips; caps pulled low; worn sneakers. I could not stop looking at a little boy, curled inside a cage on a concrete floor, under a blanket that looked like it was made of aluminum foil. He was clutching a dirty stuffed rabbit and had cried himself to sleep.

"Thank goodness we're protected," Ammi would whisper. "We followed the rules. We're just awaiting our appeal. Inshallah. It will happen."

But then came the raids. For so many months, we'd see them, late at night, squads of people coming into our buildings. One night I looked out the window and saw a van full of men who had just returned home from work, their pants stiff with paint, hoodies drawn up over their necks; delivery men, fluorescent vests and pants glowing in the dark. Their wrists were pinned behind their backs. We didn't dare go down. "Good hunting?" I heard one of the ICE guys ask with a laugh. "Yeah, a good haul," answered another.

We knew they were coming. These men and women, their vests say POLICE, but they are not police. They keep coming, like black locusts, swarming up our stairwells, through the cracks and seams of our doors, driving us out.

Chapter Four

It's so green once Lidia and I leave the city, the road like a hungry tongue, lapping up trees. Bushes foam at the sides. All this air and glaring light rushing through the windshield. How can there be so much beauty when my mother is locked up in some detention center? I hate all of it—the green fields, the wide highway, the occasional flag stabbing the big sky. That's what had us fooled about this country. We sang it at school for assembly: *This land is your land, this land is my land / From California to the New York island* . . . I believed it, as did Ammi.

I remember once we were driving to Bear Mountain and she said, "How beautiful! This place is settler country."

"Ammi!" I cried. "You're identifying with genocidal colonizers?"

She gave me a sharp look. "All I'm saying is this is a big country. Vast. Not a place of corruption and bribes. They'll find room for us."

" 'We're pointed toward the American continent,' " I quoted.

"What was that?"

"Just a book." Ammi never liked the Beats—she said they were seedy spoiled brats.

"You know I once did a paper on Walt Whitman. So generous, his vision of America." She quoted: "'Others will enter the gates of the ferry, and cross from shore to shore—'"

"I've heard that," I groaned, slumping against the door. Could I once quote something and not have to hear about her stale old stories? When Ammi saw that I'd put 'English major' for my college applications, she went to the library and dumped a bunch of her favorites on my desk: Jane Austen, George Eliot, the Brontës.

I don't see how any of Ammi's ideas about how welcoming America is could still be true. Lidia's beside me, grimly leaning into the wheel as she squints into the sun, then glances over at the GPS on the dashboard. We decided Kamal shouldn't come—he's playing video games with his friend Amir. It hasn't been easy keeping him calm. He's back to his old nervous habits—chewing on his shirt collar until it's frayed. I worry that he'll start wetting his bed again, leaving those ragged brown rings on the sheets. Without being too obvious, I'm always sniffing when he passes me, trying to catch the telltale stink. Last night as I was drifting to sleep, I heard footsteps, and then he was climbing into bed next to me. His bony ankles slid against my shins.

"Where's Ammi?"

"She had to go away."

"But why?"

I paused, thinking. "They just have a lot of questions for her."

"What questions?"

I drew a blank. "Long questions. She has to write them up. Longhand. They don't even have a computer there. And . . ." I kept going, as if rushing through a writing assignment for

English, one invention topping another. "She's taking a class. You remember her real estate classes? Well, this is an extra one."

Even in the dark I could see the skeptical crease in his brow. Still he folded into me, his belly warm against my spine, his breaths going slow until I could tell he'd fallen asleep. But I could not.

So many lies.

— — —

When Ammi shuffles into the room, my usually proud mother looks tiny. The ugly uniform they have to wear, like nurses' scrubs, swims on her. The pants hang off her hips. The V of the shirt droops to show her clavicle and the wiry muscles of her neck, since she's clipped up her unruly hair. It's rare to see her without earrings, necklace, her daub of shiny lip gloss. Her face—gaunt, as if there's a slice of flesh taken under each cheek. Her mouth twitches. Is she going to cry? Then she lifts up her chin. I do the same. That's us: proud, furious, while inside we're weeping-scared.

"Oh, Ammi," I whisper.

"Rania."

We are silent, trembling just a bit. Then her mouth pinches. "How's Kamal? Is he all right?"

A sting of anger-hurt. She's always worrying about Kamal more. He's the baby, the miracle born in this country, the citizen, our little sapling we hope will help us take root here. "He's okay."

She sighs with relief and then lapses into Urdu, nervously chatting, telling me to remember to water the plants, to check Kamal's math homework as he sometimes skips problems, watch for red around his ears since he's prone to infections. She stops. "I am so sorry, Lidia. I just, sometimes, I need to use my mother tongue."

"Of course," Lidia says softly.

We pause, awkward. I can see Lidia glancing up at the clock on the wall. She warned me that they may not let us see each other for more than a half hour, especially if there's a long line. And judging from the people squeezed into folding chairs and pressing close to the scratched plastic divider, they could cut us off soon. So Lidia fills us in on the status of the case—she's filed for a reprieve to get Ammi out; she's explained that this is an error since we are appealing, and that Ammi has the resources to post bond.

"Sadia, we need to talk about who you've authorized to watch the kids."

Now my mother truly looks small, as if she's shrinking into the folds of her cotton top.

"I thought it was Maria Auntie," I whisper.

Lidia and Ammi exchange looks.

"Maria is very sorry," Lidia says, "but when I explained that she has to go to court to enforce the guardianship, she rescinded. Her daughter is looking at a misdemeanor. Maria's afraid they'll use it as an excuse to deport them too."

"She got scared," Ammi says. "The raid, it spooked her."

Of course. I always knew they were undocumented, but it never meant anything before. Half the people in our building might not have their papers in order. But it's like everything else these days—the raids and the vans and the men in black vests; the neighbor who told me about how ICE showed up at her nephew's door on the day of his graduation—our world is un-raveling so fast. All the feints and exhausting choices we make, the doctors we don't go to, the mail we don't answer, just to stay a step ahead, it's all vanishing. We don't exist. We're not allowed to exist. Not these days.

"I can take care of my brother!" I say hotly. "I do it all the time."

"Legally not until you're eighteen."

"Rania can take care of most things." She turns to me. "You know where I keep the bank card. We're paid up on the rent through June. Utilities too. And I have enough for rent through the summer." She says this proudly.

"Is there anyone else?"

She is leaning forward, eyes blazing. "Rania, you need to find your uncle. He can sign as family."

This doesn't make sense. My family is back in Pakistan. They disowned her after her marriage.

"My uncle? You told me—"

"I know what I told you," she snaps. "You need to get to him. He is the kind one. His heart is soft, not like the others." She looks like she's going to cry.

"I don't understand—"

But she's not listening to me. "In the bottom of the hallway closet is an orange bag. You'll see it there. There's an extra bank card with the password. My address book. Find Mona's informa-tion. She may know where Salim is. About a year ago she rang me and told me she'd seen him."

This is too much, all at once. My uncle? Mona? "Ammi, please. Who's Mona? How can I talk to—"

"Rania! Focus. No time for tears. We will get through this as we always have." Her face has become hard and still.

But I see the fear in her eyes. Her will has come up against something bigger than her, bigger than all of us.

A guard steps forward. "Ma'am, there are others waiting—"

I can't help it—a sob rises up inside me.

"Rania," my mother says sharply. She offers a valiant smile, touches my hand. "Head up. We will win. Just remember what I told you." But as Lidia and I stand and gather our belongings, I see Ammi as I first saw her today: frightened and lost in a too-big uniform.

— — —

Once outside in the parking lot, I'm gulping air. All around us are families banging out of cars and little children clutching their parents' hands, balloons floating over their heads. The hills, flush with green, spread in the distance. *This is a big country,* Ammi had said. So much open land, mocking us.

"What did she mean? About my uncle?" I ask Lidia.

"It's an idea she has. Your uncle—"

"He's really in this country?" I cry.

She pauses. "Yes."

"How could I not know that?"

"Your mother had her reasons, Rania. A while ago she brought him up, said that he may be helpful in building her case. How he knew about what she'd been through and we could possibly file a statement from him."

"Do you think it will help?"

Lidia presses the key fob in her palm and unlocks the car door. "Anything is worth a try at this point."

— — —

Back at our apartment, just as I'm inserting our key, I smell a telltale, funky-wet odor. "I did not!" Kamal cries when I mention it, but I can tell, the way he chews on his T-shirt collar, that he's wet his pants. I order him to change and take a shower, then I take his clothes, strip the sheets for good measure, scoop up quarters, and go downstairs to the laundry.

One machine is churning and the other has stopped. Inside is a load of clothes, mashed in a gluey mess against the inside barrel. I check my quarters. I have just enough for our load and the dryer. But I can't wait. I've got to feed Kamal and get going on homework. Maybe I can hang the sheets and blanket to dry on the fire escape. So I drag out the other person's laundry, deposit it into the dryer, and use up half my coins on their wash.

I'm bone-tired, so I heat Kamal's supper and let him finish the last of the Oreo cookies, which he carefully splits and licks the cream inside before cramming the rest in his mouth. Thank God for Maria Auntie—she's brought over a pot of soup and milk and eggs and bread. After he's done, I make him wash his plate and then I let him climb onto my lap. He smells good—of lemony shampoo and soap. Kamal looks a lot like Ammi—he has her hair, which curls thickly at his neck and her wide-spaced cheeks, so he looks like a little lion. But he has none of her ferocity, her will. When he's unhappy, he goes glum and silent. He tucks himself away, folding up his knees at his chest.

"Ammi isn't coming home for a while," I tell him.

His little body freezes. "Why?"

"There are some problems. Remember we talked about how Ammi and I belong to Pakistan, and you were born here?"

He nods.

"So they're trying to figure that out. How all of us can stay."

"Why can't they figure it out here? In our apartment?"

I sigh. "It doesn't work that way."

Kamal bolts from my lap and stands in front of me, hands in fists, his lower lip puckered. "She has to come home! *Now!*"

Then he runs into our room and slams the door, making the wall shake. I wait a few minutes and gently tap on the door, calling softly, "You have me, right?"

His voice is muffled. "I don't like you! You're not Ammi."

A thousand cracks splinter through my body.

— — —

In the closet, I find the orange vinyl bag. Inside are silly things: a little satchel with some hair, probably mine or Kamal's. A few cheap bangles. A makeup bag and little vials of perfume. The bank card, as promised, with her code: NAVEDALWAYS444. There are also several envelopes, each with the words *In Case of Emergency.* To my surprise, they are stuffed with bills: five twenties in one, two fifties in another. Once I go through all the envelopes, I'm amazed to find six hundred dollars in cash.

Then I notice a large manila envelope filled with old photos. In one, my parents are on a motor scooter: He's got a mustache and is wearing a leather jacket and jeans. She's laughing, leaning into his back. She looks so young, as young as me.

This was my future, Ammi often told me.

But what about my future? I want to ask.

My hand touches something smooth and square. An address book, with a little tab that snaps shut. It looks very old, the leather worn. Inside, in her very neat handwriting, are so many names. Some I don't know. From years ago, back in Lahore. My family. To my amazement, they're all there—my grandparents, her brothers, their telephone numbers and addresses, their birthdays. The same for her cousins. I wonder, would it be so bad if we went back to Pakistan? Then I remember what Ammi always told me: *You have no idea what it's like to be a girl in that family, Rania. They do not bend and they do not forgive.*

All this time, she's carried these bits from all the people who turned their backs on her. Next to Salim, she wrote: *Favorite color: blue.*

Part of me wants to rip these pages out. Who cares? None of them ever helped us.

But she told me to find Mona. I remember hearing about Mona. She was a family friend who lived down the road from my grandparents, called Ammi when she settled in the US, not long ago. I page through the old names. Then I find it, in the back. No last name, just a phone number. When I call, a woman chirps on the voice mail message, "Mona here. So sorry I'm not here to take your call. I'm sure I'm on a long shift. Or not wanting to talk to you. Just kidding! You know what to do!" When the beep sounds out, I grow shy. "Mona, this is Rania. Sadia's daughter. Um, do you think you can call me back?"

I slip the photo into my pocket, put everything away, then realize the laundry was probably ready a long time ago. As I'm heading downstairs, I remember I never picked up the mail. It's nothing special—mostly flyers, a welcome from Hunter College. A small card twirls down to the floor. I pick it up: David Gonzalez. Caseworker. Child Protective Services. Scrawled across: *Contact me ASAP.*

Shoving it in with the mail pile, I go downstairs to the basement. What I put in the dryer is gone. But our own laundry is tossed out, Kamal's bright-blue-checkered sheet stretched out on the floor, and his underwear, jeans, and socks scattered. Cursing, I mash it into a soggy pile, carry it back upstairs, and drape everything on the fire escape and the small line Ammi uses. From here, I can see into Mrs. Flannery's narrow window. She is sitting at her table, eating a bowl of soup. At some point, she raises her head and looks up. Her eyes meet mine. I stare back at her, my insides quivering, and touch the photo in my pocket.

Chapter Five

"Wait for me."

That's what Abu whispered as he pushed the mosquito netting aside. I pretended to be asleep, scrunched tight in a ball, the way I liked to do, arms wrapped around my knees.

"Rania, I promise. I'll be back soon. And then we will take our trip to America."

I peeked my eyes open; my mother hovered in the doorway. She was so slender, like a girl, with her narrow hips, arms across her thin chest. I could see them, two silhouettes melting in and out as they said their goodbyes.

Years later when I saw the movie *The Incredibles,* I was sure that was who we were, a family able to stretch and jump and squeeze around any obstacle. We moved around a lot because Abu worked for different newspapers. First Lahore, then Islamabad and Karachi, my favorite, because it smelled like the sea. Later we moved to Hyderabad, and back again to Lahore. Ammi got good at setting up our flats: the plants she would line on the sill; my favorite food she knew how to cook—aloo parathas steaming off the kathi pan. Or toast and her strained yogurt and slices of papaya—she taught me how to pick the right one, squeeze the heavy, wide part to make sure it was firm and look for speckles of brown.

I knew Abu was always going off to do something dangerous—how many times had I watched him buckle his leather bag, push a cigarette pack into his pocket, and slip away, at funny hours? But he always came back. He'd sit at the table, stubbing out cigarette after cigarette, regaling us with his stories of the policeman he'd bribed to get someone to talk, or the army man who gave him a tip off the record. He'd tell me about the cars with tinted windows that followed his, or the time he walked out of his office to find his tires slashed. Ammi would smile, but it was a tired smile. She'd empty the ashtray, set down more chai, and say, "Don't frighten her, Naved. She doesn't have to know everything."

"Oh, but she does," he'd say, and grin. "She should know the nonsense we put up with to tell the truth." Later, he'd lift me onto his lap and let me tap his laptop keys. Words, magic words, spilled like starlight over my fingers. That was our special power. Stories and questions. Even when he went on an assignment like this latest one—far away, he said, to a region the government didn't want him to report about. After, we were going on a holiday, to America! Abu had an invitation to a conference, and they'd saved up enough money for us all to go. We had the plane tickets, the hotel room. Ammi promised she would take me up to the top of the Empire State Building and buy sneakers in Times Square.

For several days Abu would call, right on time, every four hours. Sometimes it was nothing: Ammi would pick up, murmur a few words, then hang up. That was their system: he always checked in with her. But the morning came when I woke and found Ammi, still in her clothes from the night before, her braid loosened like a ragged twig. There were dark, ashy circles under her eyes.

"Abu?" I asked.

She pressed her lips together, twisted around, and made me breakfast—toast sprinkled with butter and cinnamon and papaya slices. Then she took me to school and was waiting by the gate when I ran outside. Her hair had been braided, but now she wore sunglasses that she never took off. She brought me right home and then sat out on the balcony, under the swaying wash, smoking a cigarette. By evening, I heard her talking, fast, to other people. Her voice shot up and down, like the kites we used to fly on the Karachi beach. But she never cried.

And it was only later that I saw her once more, on the phone. She didn't say anything, just turned away from me, shoulders bowed. I watched her slowly set the phone down.

"Abu?" I asked. "When is he coming back?"

She twisted around. Now there were no sunglasses, just her eyes, bulging and swollen. And a wetness glistening on her face.

"He's not," she told me.

I ran from the room, flung myself down on my bed, pulled my knees close. If I shut my eyes, I told myself, he'd come back, and call out, "Good, Rania! You waited for me!" I waited and waited, so long, I fell asleep.

— — —

What happened next was fast, as if our little flat were a bottle turned upside down. Ammi whirled from room to room in broken, sobbing motions. Clothes, shawls, chappals, hairbrushes, luggage, and papers were flung on the bed. The bookcase by Abu's desk was disgorged of its files and Ammi's paperbacks from university. One of Abu's friends from the newspaper came over and tried to stop her, but she said, "We must leave, right away."

"Sadia, please! You're not in danger."

She spun around, her hair loosening from its braid. "Do you really believe that?" She flung a jacket into the suitcase. "I am not waiting around to find out. Not for me. Not for my daughter."

"But what about the investigation?" he asked.

"Investigation?" she spat back. "You are joking, hanh?"

"Yes. Naved is respected. They'll get to the bottom of this."

"'They'?" she interrupted. "You have no idea what you're talking about. If I pursue this, what do you think will happen? Some goon will show up at our door. I promise you that. You think Rania and I will be safe?"

She pointed to a suitcase. "Take that to the door."

Suddenly it was as if she remembered I was there. She kneeled down, put both hands on my shoulders. "You're my good girl, aren't you?"

I gave her a sober nod.

"This is a very special thing I am asking you. So you have to be extra special good."

Hot anger spiked through me. My mother didn't need to say this. I always took pride in how I followed instructions, how I was better than all the other children, even. Ammi loved to boast how at three I could tie my own shoelaces and knew how to read because she'd taught me. I always felt as if I were the tail of my brave mermaid mother, shimmering with shiny scales, hard and strong like her.

"We're going to the airport. And there will be people who may ask us a lot of questions. We're going to tell them that Abu isn't feeling well. He's joining us later."

"Is Abu sick?" I asked.

She bit her lip. "In a way. If they ask, we will tell them he is joining us in a day or two. We are going on ahead, to go shopping. We'll get you those sneakers you wanted."

"But Abu said he'll take me." He'd promised we'd stroll into the big stores in Manhattan and I could pick any sneakers I wanted so when we got back, I'd run faster than the chowkidar's son, who sometimes helped wash down the cars. Ammi was horrified at how I played with servants and came home with scabs on my knees, but Abu just chuckled and said, "Apple doesn't fall very far, does it?"

"Rania." Her voice was a warning.

I stomped back to my room, still confused. Was Abu gone or not gone? Every time I thought about him, I felt a tingling on my skin. I thought of the dusty corner under my bed or that space under the bathroom sink. I was always losing things—an old barrette, a doll—and Abu would help me search in those places, seizing my lost item and declaring, "See! It's un-disappeared!"

Now I had to search all by myself. I found my notebook with the sparkly cover under my bed and a novel my mother had given me in my closet. I shoved them both in my bag. I figured Ammi would run back for anything I forgot. Ammi thought of everything.

Lucky. My parents have always taught me to pay attention to words. *Lucky, lucky girl* is what my mother called me when my new gold ear stud fell out, and we found it in the courtyard. Abu laughed, then, propped me up on my shoulders and carried me around like a princess. *Lucky* again at airport security, a man inspected our passports, the two-week visas, and the letter of invitation to a conference.

"Madam, your husband?"

"He is delayed." Her grip tightened on my arm as a warning. There had been an item in the newspaper—JOURNALIST DISAPPEARS ON ASSIGNMENT. Would the man put it together?

"Just a little holiday beforehand"—her hand brushed the top of my head—"with my daughter."

The man's bushy eyebrows lifted. He looked down at our passports, then at us. Was that a twitching frown of disapproval? Then he shut the passports and waved toward the entrance. "All right then, madam. Enjoy your time."

On the flight Ammi let me watch as many movies as I wanted—she wasn't even mad that I didn't read. Most of the time, she was hunched under the thin blue blanket.

Lucky again, at immigration in JFK Airport. Ammi looked blearily at the woman behind the plastic divider who examined our passports. "The reason for your trip?" she asked brightly. She had very red lipstick.

"Work," my mother lied. "A conference."

"What kind?"

Ammi hesitated. "Communications—" Her whole body seemed to have frozen. We used to hear stories from friends about being grilled at the airport in America, coming from Pakistan. And the invitation, I knew, was folded into her purse, with Abu's name, not hers.

I stepped forward, stood on my toes. "My ammi is going to give a talk," I said. "And I'm here to listen. And buy sneakers."

The woman smiled. There was a *ch-chunk* sound of her stamping our passports.

That's when I knew: This is how we would get by. Luck and lies.

— — —

In America, holed up in the hotel, there were days when the night terrors crawled into my throat and my eyes and came streaming out of my hair. For I knew Abu was disappeared forever. I could see the bad men that had come for him. They could come for us too, yes they could, Ammi said. They were stretching and moving as shadows on a wall. They carried tire irons, like the dacoits Abu told me about, the time he trespassed on some land for a story and got chased away. Or sometimes they had long curving knives, in their teeth, like in a cartoon.

We shifted to an apartment in Brooklyn, friends of friends, who had an extra bedroom that looked out over a gray shaft. One day Ammi put on her dangling silver earrings, drew her eyes with kohl, and registered me for school—I began fourth grade, amazed I didn't need a uniform. She even got a little job helping out in a travel agency, picked up work as she could. But my terrors persisted. How could a person disappear? What happened to his jeans and his shirt, the button-down one he liked? I had nightmares of Abu lying on a road. He turned the color of dirt, reddish brown. Leaves twisted in his mouth. At night I'd hear Ammi weeping and then she'd clutch me tight in the bed. In the morning she would spring me loose to school. "You ask the teacher three important questions, Rania," she would say. "That's who we are. Who your father was. We ask questions. And we do not give up."

Ammi began to groan with sickness. She would bolt from our bed, cupping her stomach, and I'd hear her retching inside the bathroom down the hall. The wife brought her broth and torn-up bits of paratha. One day she gently laid down a slender box. Ammi took it and disappeared down the hall. When she came back, she told me, "I'm having a baby." It was Kamal, our tiny tadpole, swimming in Ammi's belly. A miracle. A sign that running was the right thing to do. A part of Abu would be born, here.

Over supper every night Ammi asked me my three questions for the teacher, and I would tell her. I wanted to know why oceans had salt and lakes did not. Why did the mothers here show up at school dressed in drab colors, but the kids could wear what they wanted—a girl in my class had on neon-pink tights! What's the difference between a barrister and a lawyer? Why do they spell *favor* without the *u*? Ammi would laugh, and in school I got little stickies of gold stars and smiley faces on my notebooks. *Rania is so lively!* the teachers would write. *So inquisitive!*

Yes, I kept asking my questions. But why we left so fast, what happened to Abu, tunneled deep into Ammi and me, in a place with no light. My questions about home stayed in an iron lockbox of memories.

Chapter Six

"Wow." It's the Monday after my visit to Ammi, a week since the ICE officers took her away. Fatima and I are in a park across the street from school, soaking in the sunshine. Fatima sits back on the bench, chugs her Sprite.

A rough day in classes—I couldn't focus most of the time and I hadn't done any of my assignments, not after seeing my mom in detention. It's like all my energy shrank and went small, the way my mother looked. In English, Ms. Ricardo said to me, "What's going on, Rania? Serious case of senioritis?" I slammed out of the classroom. If it were Mr. D from last year, he'd pull out of me what was going on. I'm not one of those kids who goes to office hours and sobs about her problems to a teacher. No way.

Fatima shakes her head. "You have an uncle? Living here?"

"Apparently."

"That is wack."

"No kidding."

"Are you going to try and find him?"

"I guess." I add, "But why should I bother? Dude didn't even call us when he moved here."

"Do you know that?"

"What do you mean?" I look at her, incredulous. "He's, like, from my mom's family. They suck. They never helped us. They just let my mom go."

"Maybe he did try to contact your mom." She tilts the can again, takes a long gulp. "After all, she lied to you about the asylum stuff."

I start. "She didn't lie."

Fatima turns to me. Her eyes are hazel, flecked with green, turning up in the corners, which makes it seem as if she's always musing, knowing better than others. "Rania, just be open. You never know."

"I do know!"

She sighs. "My mom says that when we come here, there's always so much we leave behind."

"What's that mean?"

"There's some weird shit between my mom and her sister. Her older one. Mom never calls her. But she never tells me what happened. Says it goes way back, from when they were girls. Some kind of jealousy stuff. Her sister got to go to college."

I thrust up from the bench and we start heading to the subway. I don't want to hear this. My head is rattling: about Kamal and his bed-wetting and what to make for supper, and why Mona hasn't called me back. The card from that Gonzalez guy. My school assignments. Even though there are only a couple of weeks to go, it burns to mess up my record.

Fatima turns and asks softly, "What about graduation?"

I stop, rocking back on my heels. It's the beginning of June. Graduation is in two weeks. I picture the package with my purple robe and cap and tassel tossed into our bedroom closet.

Fatima and I have already picked out our sandals—she's gone for red, and I'm wearing gold. I even get to stride up a second time for an English award. I kept imagining Ammi in the audience, her head tilted up, that pleased-but-I-knew-it expression on her face. Everything we've done—that tunnel of fright and the hectic years in a small apartment; Ammi's anxious breaths in my hair, egging me on, sleeping on my bed, and reading my books; and then her figuring out how to be an Uber driver; the accordion file with our application growing fatter; her real estate books, and so much talk about the future, like that crazy lapping road I'd felt the other day—all of it led to this pinpoint moment, walking across the stage. If I graduated, I'd told myself, that was one more notch into the future. One more assurance that we were going forward, not back. Me breaking loose, finally, no more Ammi breathing her dreams into me.

"Yeah," I say. "What about it?"

"You can still go, right?"

"Of course! Why wouldn't I?" But my voice sounds too bright as I swipe my MetroCard and push through the turnstile.

— — —

I'm digging for my key when my phone dings and shows an unfamiliar number: Jersey City. Then I remember: Mona.

But Mrs. Flannery is suddenly right next to me, glaring through her eyeglasses, which gives her an owlish look. "Where is your mother?" I can hear that old-fashioned principal voice, suspicious. Her quilted robe is snapped to her neck, but it's off by one, giving her a cockeyed look. Everything about her—the yellowed edge of her collar, the scent of stale rose and talc—makes me sad and furious. It's as if she's what's standing between me and my normal life. Whatever that is.

"I'm sorry, I have to get this—"

"Where is she?" she repeats, and takes a step closer. Her eyes are a cloudy gray green, weak. She makes me feel pinned with fright.

I swallow. "She's working."

"I see what's going on! Your mother isn't there! I saw, in the night."

The phone bleats. "Please, Mrs. Flannery. I have to get this."

"Criminal!"

"Please," I beg.

"She's a criminal. You all are!" She shuffles off.

The phone has quieted in my pocket. Mrs. Flannery has slammed her door, clinking the chain on the other side. I'm so relieved Kamal is on a playdate with Amir. Once inside the apartment, I can't stop trembling. Ammi always told me, *She's a lonely person. Her daughter never visits her. She's letting it out on us.*

I press Mona's number. "Hullo!" she greets me cheerily.

"It's Rania."

"Oh yes! So sorry about taking so long. I work a long shift and I always forget to charge my phone. What can I do for you, Rania?"

I'm taken aback. I'd worked up this conversation so many times in my head I thought for sure she knew who I was and what had happened to Ammi, and would offer me a solution. I thought she'd sound familiar, like family, folding me in.

"I . . . My mother told me to call you. I'm looking for my uncle. Salim?"

There's a long pause. Too long, drawing between us. My ribs tighten.

"Rania, the thing is this—"

"Do you know where he is?" I interrupt.

Again another pause.

"Please," I beg. "My mother—"

"Where is your mother?" she asks sharply.

It's my turn to pause. I haven't said it out loud to anyone except for Fatima. If I don't say it, maybe it isn't true. "She's—they've taken her into detention. Immigration."

"Oh dear." I can hear the sorrow in her voice. "Poor Sadia."

No! I want to shout. Ammi is never *Poor Sadia*. Never. She would hate such words used about her. It takes all my effort not to hang up. Tears fleck thickly on my lashes and I blink them away.

"You are alone?"

"My brother is with me."

"You have a brother?" She sounds surprised.

"Yes. Kamal." I add, "He was born here. He's eight."

"I see." She seems to be weighing something. In the background I can hear plates clattering. This is my life, I want to say, and you're putting dishes away?

"It's messed up," I say. "This whole country is messed up right now."

She laughs. "I see you have Sadia's spunk."

"Ammi always said I more take after Abu. He was tall."

"Is that right?" There's a funny tone in her voice.

54

The way she comments—skeptical, questioning—makes me tense. We don't talk about Abu too much, not with anyone outside me and Kamal. And after our first year or two, Ammi began to avoid anyone from back home. I remember there were phone calls in the middle of the night, and someone who knew Abu would come visit, a fellow journalist, to see how we were doing. They were always kind and funny, asking about school and friends, staring at the framed photo of Abu Ammi keeps on a shelf, and offering to help. She politely served them snacks and chai but she never called them. Maria Auntie, your friends, she often told me, they're your new family.

"So," I say. "My uncle. Salim?"

"Right." She clears her throat. "He came here . . . I think it was two, three years back. At least that's what I'd heard. He had a job, for a bank. He was married, you know—"

"No, I don't know."

"They both came, with the children, who were quite young, I think."

"But what about my mother? Why didn't he call her? Call us?"

"From what I understand, he tried. But she . . ." She hesitates. "She wouldn't speak to him."

I drop down on the sofa, stunned. That makes no sense. How many times did I hear Ammi cry behind a closed door, about how hard-hearted her family was? How they had cut her out? I'd feel a swoop in my own chest, as if I was falling with her, into a lonely hole. No light, only those mean relatives who hurt me too.

"Look, I think Salim had his own troubles. He was married, but the girl, she wasn't doing too well with the immigration.

They made the best of it, I suppose. If your mother was going to do her thing—"

"What thing?" I ask, suddenly hostile. I sense gossip wreathed around Ammi. That's what she always said—growing up, she couldn't bear the chatter and nasty rumors.

"I'm sorry. I shouldn't have said that. Your mother, I met her only a few times. I knew Salim better. He was a few years older than me. But I remember hearing . . . she was such a free spirit."

"That doesn't sound like a compliment."

"Ah, sharp, like Sadia," she remarks.

I wince.

"I remember your grandparents," she continues. "They were so sweet. We used to play in their big garden. My brother, one day, he was climbing up the tree that is next to their house, and your grandfather, he was so stern! We all were afraid of him. He was retired but we could see he was still a general. So my brother climbed up and crawled onto the limb that went right next to your grandfather's window. We were sure he would yell at him. But then suddenly the shutter flapped open and there he was! Not stern at all, but laughing and he told my brother to keep climbing and he could come in through the window."

She stops when she can hear me crying. Not big-deal crying, just sniffles and hot tears sliding down my cheeks. I never do that in front of strangers.

"I am so sorry, Rania. That was wrong of me. These family feuds. They are hard on everyone."

Who are all these people? I think. A whole world that knew my grandparents, that made judgments about us? Why didn't

I know Mona, just across the river, in New Jersey? And I have cousins, here?

"Do you know where my uncle is now?"

"I heard he was in Connecticut somewhere. But I don't have an address."

I slump back on the cushions. Why did I even call her just to hear stories that make me feel bad about all I don't have? And yet, sitting on the sofa where Ammi usually pulls out her bed, sun streaming on the floor, I feel a nub of warmth in Mona, of connection.

Her voice brightens. "There is one possibility. Hema Auntie. She knows everybody. And I think Salim may have stayed with her in the beginning. Hold on, I'll call her on the landline right away."

I can hear her set the phone down, then she's making pleasantries, and lowers her voice. I pluck out a word or two: "Sadia," "better you see her," and "no, no expectations." When she comes back to me, she tells me to write down an address in Wayne, New Jersey. "Tomorrow," she says. "Eleven o'clock."

I want to say, "I have school," but she adds firmly, "Hema Auntie will be waiting for you."

After the call, I make my plan: I'll drop Kamal at school, then drive to New Jersey. It means cutting classes but what else can I do? Kamal can go home with his friend Derek if I'm late. I go downstairs, move Ammi's car, since there's alternate parking tomorrow, then heat up Maria Auntie's soup, sit with Kamal while he does his homework, oversee his bath, and put him to bed. Fatima texts me several times but I shut off the phone, finish my missed assignments, and hand them in electronically. *Sorry, Ms. Ricardo,* I write. *I can't be in school tomorrow. Doctor's appointment.* Then I shut the light off.

How easy it is to lie.

— — —

The next morning, after I've dropped off Kamal, I sit in the car and stare at the scrap of paper with Hema Auntie's address. Great. I have to go see some auntie who is going to give me the once-over. Who lives at least an hour and a half away. I slam into reverse, swerve away from the curb. A car horn blares. Suddenly I'm scared. It seems like ages ago that Fatima and I were wearing our FREEDOM T-shirts and waltzing up the stairs to school, arms linked.

I'm furious at those people in quilted vests.

At my mother, for all her secrets.

At everyone, for stealing my last days of high school.

I clutch the wheel and steer through traffic to the entrance of the Belt Parkway. The Verrazano bridge looms, spires glinting. I swallow, tightening my grip. I've never driven across a bridge or so far.

I hunch forward to merge carefully, making my way across Staten Island, then exiting onto I-95 through New Jersey. This is more highway driving than I've ever done. The route climbs up and up curving roads until I park in front of a big white brick house. There's a hissing sound of a sprinkler, somewhere behind the big hedges. At the door I catch myself in the narrow glass—wrinkled shirt, lace-up boots, hair a mess. I feel like a bike messenger, grimy, carrying the stink of New York City streets.

When I press the bell, the ringtone sounds inside a huge space. The door opens and I'm greeted by an older woman— hawk-nosed, a streak of white in her hair, which swings at her chin. She's wearing a blue kurta over white slacks, gold slip-on sandals. "You must be Rania!" I feel her eyes raking me up and down. "Come in, come in!" she urges.

I follow her, clicking down the polished hall floor, past the ornate furniture, just beyond huge windows that look out onto the shimmering blue of a swimming pool. In the large kitchen, a woman at the sink—the maid—is waved away. A tray of tea and sandwiches has been set out for me.

"Please, please, eat." She laughs. "We still have so much food left over from the iftar. I have chicken cutlet? Biryani?"

My stomach scrapes hollow. In the rush to get Kamal to school I never ate breakfast. But something about Hema Auntie makes me uneasy. As if I'm a beggar, grubby with need. I grab one half sandwich and cram it down, quick.

"This is perfect, thanks," I say.

"So tell me," she says, pouring the tea. "You are how old?"

"Seventeen," I reply. "I'm just about to graduate."

"Ah." She smiles. "My son is at UPenn. Premed. You are going where?"

I get it—time to trot out credentials. "Hunter," I tell her. When it doesn't register, I say, "The honors college. I got a scholarship."

She nods absently. Clearly she's not impressed. All those fancy schools—UPenn, Brown, Vassar—were out of the question for me. I was going to apply, and then I deleted them from my list. It would be too hard for Ammi to keep up our household without me and we could never afford those tuitions. This is what I want: to stay with Fatima. To walk the blocks I know, past men scraping spiny fruit by the curb; to stop off for noodles at Lucky Eight and sit in Sunset Park; I want to talk and dream and complain. Why can't I do what other kids do?

She peppers me with more annoying questions, but I'm still starving, so I mumble answers as I take another half sandwich. Her look is sharp, assessing. When I fumble my way to Ammi's situation—delicately mentioning we're having issues with immigration—her nod grows more vigorous. "Oh yes. We'd heard Sadia had some trouble. Things did not go as planned."

"What do you mean?" The sandwich turns dry in my mouth.

"The hearing? Is that what they call it?" Her look now is haughty.

"I guess."

"It must have been such a disappointment. I don't know much about these matters. We came a while ago. My husband's position . . . I'm sure you've heard. He's head of pulmonary medicine at Hackensack."

I swallow hard. I didn't even know Hema Auntie existed before yesterday. But there's something about her that reminds me of Ammi—an air of *we are important*.

"Salim Uncle?" I prompt.

She gets up, rummaging in a desk drawer, and lifts out a small bundle bound with a rubber band. "I don't have a phone number, but I do have this mail for him. It just came a few weeks ago, even though he hasn't been here for quite a while. I've been meaning to send it off." She plucks off a sticky note. "That's his address."

I look down at an address in Stamford. My heart starts to quicken. "He's still there?"

"I believe so. He had a position with RBS. Last I heard there were some problems . . ." Sitting down again, she scrapes her chair closer. Her eyes are a gray green. Her hands are on mine, ringed fingers glinting. "If you like, I could contact your family. I'm sure they'd be happy to be of help—"

"No!" Then, remembering my manners, I say, "Thank you so much, Auntie. You've been very kind. I should get back to my brother." I stand, point to the bundle. "Can I take this?"

Her smile drops. "Yes, of course." Her voice is cold.

I hurry down the steps, my bag banging at my hip, relieved to get out of there. I can't explain it: something felt wrong, like a trap. Those gray-green eyes, judging. The way my throat closed shut.

My uncle, I think, dropping the packet of mail on the passenger seat. I would find my uncle. And make everything right.

Chapter Seven

"It was weird," I tell Fatima two hours later. On my way back from New Jersey, I stopped at her house in Bay Ridge, and we're sitting on her stoop. Occasionally one of her little brothers' heads pop into the front bay window—they're bouncing on the sofa. "I felt Mona and Hema Auntie gave me this whole chase. Just to, like, check me out." I shudder. "Ugh. I hated them."

"Families are weird. Mine is completely nuts."

"These people aren't even family."

"You know what I mean."

"But all this time, they knew about me. About my mom. Her hearing, what happened. How come I didn't know they even exist?"

"I guess your mom doesn't like them."

Fatima's trying to help, but inside the Elawady house, with its big, ornate furniture, she's snug inside her family. Even with all the chaos—her noisy brothers, her father yelling in Arabic at someone from his business, relatives dropping by, poor Mrs. Elawady trying to serve the meal—I feel a burn of resentment.

"I could ask my mom if she'd sign the paper about guardianship. It's not a big deal, right?"

"Maybe. But let me find out more first." Since Ammi has put in my mind this idea of an uncle, I keep seeing a door opening and a soft-faced uncle welcoming us. And cousins, for me and Kamal. Was such a normal scene possible? Back in Pakistan we mostly saw my parents' friends—from university or Abu's newspaper colleagues. They are our family, Ammi would insist. They would sit around our living room, talking all at once, going out onto the balcony to smoke. In the morning I'd find full ashtrays on the floor, or maybe a friend of Abu's sleeping the night off on the sofa.

"It's so confusing. Ammi made it seem like everything was under control. Why would she lie?"

"She wasn't lying."

"What do you call it?"

"I don't know. Maybe she had her reasons—"

There's a rattling noise on the window. We both turn to see her brothers, waving wildly, making faces. Fatima sighs. "They never leave me alone."

"They're cute."

Smiling, she nudges her shoulder into mine. "I'll tell you who's cute." Then she talks about how Jamal—the boy on the basketball court—wants her to come to a graduation party at his house—half the senior class is going. She's got an elaborate story worked up to tell her parents: about how it's a makeup session for graduation, for all the girls, and we're going to do each other's hair, and she wants me to back her up.

"Fa-Fa," I warn, "if your dad finds out, you are really screwed. He'll put you on the next flight to Cairo and you'll have a husband ASAP."

"But—"

"You remember what happened last time?"

Fatima is always getting in trouble. Once we snuck out to a party where she drank beer and danced and danced, swinging her wild hair. I dragged her back to her neighborhood, the two of us walking round the block until she could stand properly. Mr. Elawady was furious at me.

"Go!" he shouted.

"But it's late!" Fatima cried. "She needs a ride!"

I called Ammi, who picked me up after an Uber shift. "Men are like that," she said when I told her what happened. She didn't yell at me at all for being at a party with drinking. "Fatima's rebelling because he cracks down on her so much." She set her hand on mine. "You are a good friend to her."

Now Fatima rests her head on my shoulder. I breathe in her minty-coconut shampoo smell. "You're right, Rania. What would I do without you?"

What would I do without you too? I think. But I can't stop the spinning motion inside me. What if everything tilts so fast, we'll be pulled apart?

A black car pulls up to the curb and her father gets out, slamming the door. I tense. He's a thick-limbed man, with rumpled hair like Fatima, and an angry air. Fatima says it's just because he's got too many responsibilities with the business and all his relatives wanting something from him. "Fatima! Why aren't you inside, helping your mother?"

She sets her mouth into a hard line. "Just a little lie about the party," she whispers, her fingers brushing mine.

Lies, I think. Big, little lies. What are the ones that matter?

Later, back at the apartment, I'm doing my homework when the bedroom door creaks open and Kamal sidles up to me, climbs onto my lap, and sets his head on my shoulder. He rarely does that. "When is Ammi coming home, Aapi?" he asks. Only sometimes does he call me big sister.

"Soon," I say.

"Soon when?"

I don't answer, but hold him tighter until he softens with sleep and slips away, back to bed. I am left with an ache in my bones, as if I have the flu. I'm wide-awake. I pace the apartment. Ammi rarely allowed us to touch on the past. I'd ask all kinds of questions—remember that girl I used to walk to school with and who was allergic to avocadoes? Or the ice cream place across the road that had the best pistachio flavor? Sometimes she'd get a little sentimental and we'd curl up on the sofa, watch silly Bollywood movies or sing ghazals.

Rahiye ab aisī jagah chal kar jahāñ koī na ho
ham-suḵẖan koī na ho aur ham-zabāñ koī na ho
be-dar-o-dīvār sā ik ghar banāyā chāhiye

Let's live in that place where there's no one, let's go
Where no one knows our tongue, there's no one to speak to.
We'd build a house without doors and walls . . .

She'd slip her arm around me, squeeze tight. "See, Rania? That's what we are. A house without doors and walls. We have

65

ourselves. And that's enough." She'd slap her knees. "Come! No more dwelling in the past. We are here now. Remember that."

I open the closet and dig out the manila envelope I found a few days before. More photographs scatter out. There's one of my mother, not as I ever saw her. Her hair is feathered into waves, her thick blue eyeshadow matches her shalwar kameez, and a gauzy scarf floats across her neck. Her shoulders are hunched, her chest caved in. There are other people in a room, holding drinks and plates of food. It seems like a happy occasion, but she's staring right at the camera, unsmiling.

— — —

"Rania?" Lidia looks startled.

It's early the next day, and I'm sitting on a cold floor, leaning against the wall outside Lidia's office, nursing a cup of coffee when she arrives. "I need to talk to you," I say.

"Come on in." Balancing files and an overstuffed bag, she pulls out a clump of keys and lets me in. Once inside, she snaps on the lights, leads me down the hall to her room. "What can I do for you?"

Why do people keep asking that? As if it isn't obvious. Get my mother out of detention. Stop this crazy tornado of events. "Tell me about the hearing. Why didn't it go well?"

Lidia pulls off her jacket and motions to sit. Outside, I can hear the phone starting its frantic bleating. Her assistant pops her head in the door. "You've got the eight o'clock?"

"Just tell the others they'll have to wait."

Her assistant is puzzled—I'm sure there's a long line of phone appointments and people waiting. I'd called yesterday to try to squeeze myself in, but was told Lidia was booked and in court all afternoon. I decided that the only way would be to have Maria Auntie drop off Kamal at school while I headed to Lidia's downtown. Another day missed at school, but it's the last week.

"Look, Rania. You're really smart. I bet you've been taught all about how we're a nation of immigrants. Maybe you did some class trip to the Statue of Liberty. But immigration law is not the same as the rest of our legal system. You think there is some kind of fairness. But it can boil down to one judge. One guy who may be cranky or inclined to say no to ninety percent of his cases."

"And in my mother's case?"

She sighs. "I told her. That it's not always the story of what happened to you. It's the story the judge wants to hear. The problem with your case always was that it was your father who was explicitly in danger."

"That's not true! My dad disappeared! I remember, we had to flee, really fast—"

"Yes, the situation was terrible. You should see all the country information we put into the case file. How Pakistan at the time was one of the worst places for journalists. The stats are awful. But your mother was not the one targeted. We tried to get statements from family and colleagues, but it went nowhere. There never was a legitimate threat against her."

I give the desk a hard kick. "I was there! It was really scary!"

Lidia angles her head, surprised. "You remember?"

I stop kicking. *Do* I remember? I hear the sound of a gate, scraping. Hakim, the chowkidar, his face folded with fear. Abu's scooter, bumping down with a hiss. Something wrong with the tires. I rub my eyes. There's nothing more. Just that blank box where we put our old life.

"Something," I say. "Maybe a gate?"

She sits up, taut. "Yes?"

A wriggling sensation in my stomach. I swallow. A taste of strawberry. But then another blank hole. "That time was such a blur."

"You were young. Besides, there was also how your mother dressed for the hearing."

"Oh my God, isn't that completely sexist?"

"I told her. Dress down. No makeup. Maybe wear a plain sweaterdress. Look . . . innocent. When it came time for her to appear, she looked proud. She thought it was an interview for a job. They wanted her humble. And your mother isn't humble."

"My mother didn't look grateful enough."

She nods.

I hunch in my chair. "That is so messed up."

"You should have heard the government lawyers. They pressed her on everything, to prove that she was privileged. How she had a servant, part time. How she was educated. How her family was well-to-do."

"Family!" I spat the word.

"Look, it was a lousy outcome. We were assigned a judge with an eighty percent turndown rate. We immediately applied for an appeal. We got an extension. And then . . ." Lidia trails off, eyes glistening.

The noise outside, in the office, swells up. "We had an election. Your mother was unlucky."

We're supposed to be lucky. I'm supposed to be lucky. "That's it?" I ask.

"I'm afraid so."

"But that's unfair!"

"Everything has changed under this administration," she continues. "Some days I don't know what is up, what's down. The rules keep changing. I've got long-term clients in detention. I've got grandmothers put on airplanes without saying good-bye. People with job offers unable to get here. Every day it's another story. Your mother's story is just one of them."

— — —

When I step outside, it's as if a curtain has been ripped back: the muggy air, the buildings, and the people surging to the subway are a thick, stony wall. Not letting us in. I think about Hema Auntie's house, the hedges and the shimmering pool. Why isn't that possible for us? All our wily luck, remaking ourselves here, in this place we learned to seize as ours, without Abu. I belong here, in New York: in a subway car, jammed next to everyone else headed somewhere—a thousand lives, a thousand possibilities. Now I have slammed up against something hard, ungiving.

I kick and kick a low concrete wall until my toes are throbbing.

Sitting in a subway car later, Lidia's conversation gnaws at me. I unwrap my new notebook and start jotting thoughts, memories. Something about that gate in our building in Lahore. It wobbled and screeched against concrete. Hakim let me help him soap down the cars, dunking the big sponge in a pail of sudsy water. He kept pictures of his family taped to the little booth. He was missing two teeth in the front. His hands felt like leather but they were kind. Where were we going? Ice cream. Pistachio, my favorite, at the shop across the street. But no. A smudge of a man so big, his shoulders block Hakim.

I'm so busy chasing down fragments, scribbling, when the doors ding, I realize I've almost missed my stop. Grabbing my bag, I rush out, to make my last classes. I don't have a chance to hang with Fatima, but as the last bell rings, I rush again, to get to Kamal's school on time.

When he bursts out of the doors, clutching his Machu Picchu project under one arm. We three worked for hours on it, carefully laying strips of newspaper and paste, then Ammi and me watching as he painted the model. Now his whole face is lit up. His friends josh him and he spins a few times, laughing. My heart wrenches. I've got to keep him away from all the bad news, somehow.

The phone rings; there's a hollow rushing noise, then a woman asking if I'll accept charges from Sadia Hasan. Ammi! My chest starts knocking. I remember what Lidia said, about all those other clients. What if it's my mother, saying goodbye? What if she's heading to a plane? I accept the call; Ammi sounds like her usual, brusque self. "Have you found your uncle? Did you speak to Mona?"

I glance at Kamal, indicate we should stop and pull away a few feet. "I did but she didn't know anything. She sent me to Hema Auntie—"

"You went to Hema's?" She sounds angry.

"She's the one who had Salim's address. Why are you so mad?"

There's a tugging on my arm. It's Kamal, impatient.

"Wait!" I tell him. I turn back to Ammi. "Who are all these people? Why didn't you tell me about—"

"Let me speak to Kamal."

I thrust the phone into his hand. "Here, talk to Ammi."

He takes the phone from me. I watch him nod and tell her about the party in his class and the chocolate cake they ate and how his teacher said his project was awesome. "When are you coming back?" he asks. He listens, grinning in a secret, happy way, then he hands back the phone and tells me, "Ammi says she is going to get me a new Transformer."

"When?"

"Soon."

I take the phone from him. "Ammi, you can't tell him things like that."

"I'm calling for something else. I don't have much time—someone else needs to use the phone." Her voice lowers. "In the closet, inside that big bag I told you about, there's another little velvet one. Just look. You'll find it."

"What?" I roll my eyes even though she can't see. Ammi with her zippered compartments, her secrets.

"Jewelry. You can take it to Mr. Mehta. He's at Seeta Jewelers, on Coney Island Avenue. Near where we used to live. He knows me. He will give you a good price. He won't cheat you."

"I don't understand. Ammi, I was just talking to Lidia—"

"Rania, listen to me. Get what you can for the jewelry. That will hold you over for a while." There's a rattling sound in the background. "I can't call very often. My phone isn't charging right. And it's costly to use theirs. And they can use it against me. Write me and send me a phone card. You can get the address from Lidia."

"But, Ammi—"

"I have to go. I love you. Hugs and kisses to Kamal." Then she clicks off.

— — —

Great. Who do I see in front of our building, but Mrs. Flannery, sitting on a folding chair. Sometimes she puts on an outfit, maybe the kind she used to wear when she was a principal, blazers with puffy shoulders and flat shoes, and she sits there, surveying the kids walking home bowed down with backpacks, the little ones tumbling off yellow school buses, hands fluttering with construction-paper drawings, the women pushing their carts piled high with paper towels and groceries, their children trailing behind in a row, like a colorful kite tail. Kamal's got his end-of-year art project under one arm and a Popsicle in the other.

"How old are you?" Mrs. Flannery asks him when we reach the steps.

"Eight," he replies.

"Is that right?" Her glasses flash for a moment. Then she stares at me. "How is your mother?"

"She's fine," I say with a snarl in my voice. I can't help myself; I start to lie. "She has this really important job interview. To be head of a school."

Mrs. Flannery stares at me blankly. "So she's not home yet?"

I can see Kamal's face crumple. Orange from his Popsicle drips down his wrist.

"Good day, Mrs. Flannery," I say, and pull Kamal through the door.

Upstairs I usher Kamal into the apartment and then I march down the hall and press Maria Auntie's buzzer, hard. Why can't they help us? Be our standby guardians? Why does my life have to be ruined because of screwup Lucia?

The door swings open. It's Lucia. She looks exhausted and is wearing an apron spattered with tomato sauce. I remember that Maria Auntie is making her work all the time since they have to pay for a lawyer. "Yeah?" she asks.

"Forget it." I turn away.

— — —

Dinner is rushed: I overcook the chunks of meat, make soggy rice, bang the plates on the table. It's too much: the talk with Mona, the meeting with Hema Auntie. The meeting with Lidia. And my mother's call. Maria Auntie drops by to give us two yogurt containers filled with soup. She hands them to me like a peace offering. I stand there stiff, not sure what to say.

"Rania, I am so sorry. But you understand. When your mother first came to me, I said of course. But now, with Lucia's troubles . . ."

I see how hard it is for her. "It's okay, really." Though it isn't.

"I hear you have an uncle!" she says brightly. "Oh! I forgot the flan. I'll have Lucia drop it off. I have to leave for my shift."

"Flan!" Kamal shouts. Flan always makes Kamal happy—he says it's like swallowing down sunshine.

She gives me a hug. "I'm so sorry," she says, smoothing a palm on my hair.

Exhausted, I flop down on the sofa, to think. On Saturday I

can drive up to Stamford. Maybe Kamal can hang with Amir. I still can't believe this is happening to us. I've read all the headlines and watched the news about the awful stuff at the border. One evening we were cooking together with the TV on, when Ammi turned to me and said, "Just so you're clear: We're not undocumented, Rania. We are asylum seekers. There's a difference."

I remember being outraged at the time. "But what about those other families?"

She tilted up her chin, stared straight ahead. "It's a waiting game. That's all."

I wonder, after what Lidia told me about her hearing, if that is true? Are we so different?

Just as I'm about to check on Kamal, there's a soft knock on the door. Then firmer. I figure it's Lucia with the flan. But when I swing open the door, a woman I don't know is standing there. Behind her a man, shifting on his feet.

"Rania Hasan?" When I nod, she offers a smile. "May I come in, dear?"

My fingers are stiff on the knob. "You are?"

"Mr. Gonzalez."

I pull back. "Who?"

The woman answers, "We left a card the other day?"

The card. I'd tossed it on the stack of mail, tried to push it away, like everything else.

"We received word that two minors are living here without a guardian."

A slow burn as I realize: Mrs. Flannery. Her door, down the hall, shut. "It's a mistake," I start to say, but the man steps forward. He's thickly built, like the woman, only bald, and he suddenly reminds me of one of those guys in a TV show. I half expect him to start throwing tarps over the furniture and stretching yellow tape across the doorway. But it's not a crime scene.

"My uncle," I plead. "I'm going to see him this weekend."

The woman gives me a gentle smile. "You can straighten that out at the shelter."

Shelter. The word knocks into me, like a block of ice.

They're actually very kind, as kind as they can be. The woman and I go into the bedroom and talk softly with Kamal, who starts chewing on his collar but lets me fill his backpack with his favorite Transformer toys. The man, Mr. Gonzalez, has brought an old-fashioned yo-yo and he squats down before Kamal and distracts him, his wrist bending up and down, the round disc winking with tiny lights.

My eyes swing around the apartment. I take it all in—the clay pots with spider plants on the sill, our small sofa covered with an embroidered throw, the TV on the beat-up table. I keep saying, "We have an uncle. I have family," even though I'm not sure, and the woman puts her arms around me and says, "Dear, it will just be for a few days, until it's sorted out."

I don't know why I believe her.

— — —

Now my muscles know just what to do, every part of me springing to life: Pull out the luggage tucked under my bed, the one with the safety pin on the zipper. Fold up the quilt. Grab whatever is nearest—phone, laptop, books, headphones—and stuff it into my backpack. Don't linger on the Nelson Mandela poster over my bed or the photo strip with Fatima tacked to my mirror, the carnival beads draped on its rim from a school Mardi Gras. Text Maria, tell her to water the plants and move the car. Text Fatima and say I can't meet her at the subway tomorrow morning. Grab the jacket I bought from the Jamaican guy. My lace-up black boots, my Converse sneakers, my flip-flops. My graduation robe and cap, in their plastic. Maybe at some point we can come back for the rest.

There is just me and my brother following them out, hurrying down the stairs, Kamal tripping on his Nike slides, me careful not to bang the rolling wheels. We take only what our arms can hold, as if stripping down to the essence of ourselves. I've done this before: in Pakistan, when Abu disappeared. Turning myself light, thin as a shadow that can slip through a door crack, the seams of night, the corners of a neighbor's eyes.

We pull open the front door into a muggy evening. I feel like I'm some kind of story in the newspaper. That smudge at the edge before you turn the page.

I keep thinking: *This is not us.*

Manhattan, NYC

Chapter Eight

We're lucky.

They keep Kamal and me together at the shelter, in a narrow room that just barely fits a bunk bed and two thin metal lockers, where we stuff most of our belongings. I let Kamal sleep on top, to make it like an adventure. I tell him about the train I once took, from Karachi to Lahore, how it had three bunks that swung down from the wall, each one with a curtain that pulled shut. In the morning, when we stopped at a station, there was a rattling cart outside, and a man handed us milky chai through the window. I loved that trip so much that Ammi used to play a train game with me—she'd line up the dining chairs in a row and then we'd pack a little zippered bag with clothes, a midday meal of parathas and potatoes and pistachio shortbread. I sat in the front seat, my stuffed monkey on my lap, and she would sit behind, pointing out the imaginary sights. *See the wheat fields,* she'd say. *See the sunflowers bending toward us, like sunny faces!* I loved my mother most then, for she made me see the world as a place to name and conquer.

"Can we go on a trip?" Kamal asks.

"Yes," I tell him. "Very soon."

Soon he is melting-soft with drowsiness and I climb back down to my bed. But I can't sleep. I lie there, rigid on the thin mattress, alert to strange sounds: a steel door slamming. Footsteps. Children crying. The low calming voice of a grown-up. We are somewhere in Manhattan—I figured out that much from the drive—and in my mind I'm trying to sort out all the bus and train routes we'll have to take for school. And how I'm going to get people to see we don't belong here.

I wake to a gray light and someone is knocking on the door, telling us to wash up, because breakfast is downstairs in half an hour.

"Wait!" I call.

The woman pops her head in. She looks tired, impatient.

"This is a mistake. We're not supposed to be here. I need to talk to the person in charge."

"Later." She points to two white towels and a bar of soap on a chair.

We take our toothbrushes and wash up down the hall. Then we make our way downstairs, to a room with long tables and aluminum benches, where they serve us buttered toast and scrambled eggs that taste like jiggly rubber. I keep looking for an adult I can explain our situation to, but mostly it's kids of all ages, little ones swinging their legs off their chairs, others climbing up and down, and up again. The din of voices, most of them in Spanish.

A girl about Kamal's age is sitting opposite us. Her sleek black hair is done into two braids, showing a round face, her eyes two dull buttons. She doesn't say a word but stares at Kamal drinking his orange juice. "What?" he keeps asking, annoyed, but she says nothing, just keeps staring.

"She doesn't talk," someone says.

I turn to see a boy, about my age, slender, with a shock of dyed gold hair. He's got on a denim jacket and hoodie, jeans with frayed holes, done just so. He's pushed his tray away and is drawing with a pencil on a sketch pad, his wrist moving swift and sure. It's a portrait, I realize, of the little girl.

"That's good," I comment.

"I know."

Not exactly lacking in confidence, I think.

He does a few more strokes, scrutinizes it for a second, then rips the page out and hands it to the girl. "Rosa, mira." She takes it, her eyes growing wide. A grin creeps up in her mouth. Clutching the paper to her chest, she twists off the bench and runs off. He swivels to face us. "I make her one every day." He sizes us both up. "You guys are new."

"Yes." I put my hand on my brother's head. "I don't think we're staying, though. It's just some kind of mix-up."

He gives me a rueful look and starts laughing. "Yeah, right."

"You don't believe me?"

"I believe you. Don't get so mad."

"I'm not mad. I just have to find out who to talk to." I stand, scanning the noisy room.

"Good luck," he calls as I unwind from the bench.

I go from adult to adult, but they all shake their heads. "We're just aides," they say. No one seems to have any information. Back at the table I can see the boy is trying not to smirk. "Go ahead, say it. I was wrong," I say.

"You just have to be patient."

"I don't have time," I grumble.

Something about this boy makes me push back. He's good-looking, in an unusual way: slender features and long fingers; a slow, sly smile. But he's also arrogant. On the inside of his wrist is a tattoo—what look like two blue fish, swimming into each other. When I look over again, he's drawing something else. I start to untangle myself from the bench and tap Kamal that it's time to go. There's a tearing sound; the boy has ripped off another page and handed it to me. Then I realize it's a quick sketch of me—my hair wild, a squint, and my chin pushed out, stubborn.

"We'll call this one 'Impaciente.' Impatient."

I snatch it from him, face burning.

"Carlos," he says, grinning. "Me llamo Carlos."

— — —

There's a rhythm to this place, kindness and prison. But no one will talk to me, let me explain my story. Social workers patrol the hall, pulling the little kids into all kinds of activities: dance and drawing and kickball in the courtyard, then a lunch of greasy macaroni and cheese, and the lounge area, where the TV is left on. It's hard not to notice the chain on the fence and the front doors, which you can only get in when the receptionist sees you through a camera and buzzes. While Kamal and I are resting in our room with the door open, I see a trail of children, maybe five or six, walk down the hall. When they see us, they turn away, some of them throwing up their arms to hide their faces. My insides flinch. Where did they learn to do that?

Finally, I can't stand it anymore—I run down the stairs and

barge into the director's office. "You have to do something!" I cry. "We're not like these kids! We live here!"

The director, Ms. Kaplan, rises from her seat. "You need to cool down. Then I'll talk to you."

I drop down on a chair and try to suck down my anxious breaths. *Rania, you go from zero to ten like really fast,* Fatima always says. *Try to chill down to a five.* When I've calmed, I tell her my name and explain, "This whole thing is just a mistake. We're not supposed to be here."

"It's not so simple."

"But I have to go to school! I have graduation!" I add bitterly, "I've got a *life!*"

Her voice is low, firm. "Don't you think all these children had lives?"

I hunch in the chair, ashamed.

"Rania, I'm sorry. This whole situation is a mistake. We're not even the correct agency for these kids and these two populations shouldn't be mixed. Children wrenched from their parents. Their parents deported. Lawyers calling me nonstop, trying to track down relatives."

"I have an uncle," I say softly.

She scribbles this down. "Do you want to call him?"

"I don't know his number. I have an address . . ." My voice fades. I'd tried hunting him down on the internet, but there were four people with the same name in Connecticut alone. And no phone numbers.

"Anyone else who could provide standby guardianship? Or sponsorship?"

I think for a moment. "My best friend? Her mom might be able to do it."

"I suggest you call. Though now that you're in the system it's a lot more complicated."

"Complicated?"

"It's not just signing a paper. There will have to be a social worker visit and an interview with all the adults in the household, especially if they're not relatives. If they agree, they have to appear before a judge." She taps her pen on the desk. "If your mother had only taken care of this before, it could have been avoided."

Before? Ammi always tries to take care of everything—right down to telling me to buy her a phone card, which I still have yet to do. Maria Auntie just got scared. We're all scared.

"What about school?" I ask. "You can't keep me from that."

She sighs. "I wish I could send you. We're so understaffed. And we can't let you go unaccompanied. It's just about a week of official classes left."

My week. My last week of high school.

Numb, I make my way out of her office and call Fatima. I can hear the rush of people hurrying in the corridors. "Cut it out, Omar!" she yells. I'm stung with envy: something so normal, it's out of reach for me. Then I quickly tell her everything that's happened and beg her to ask her mother to sign the paper.

"Of course," she whispers. A bell bleats on her end. "I gotta go."

"Please. I have to get out of here."

"I promise. Hold tight, Ra-Ra."

Kamal and I go back to our room and lie on our bunk beds. It's hot in the room, the air thick as flannel, making me listless. My phone buzzes, showing an unknown number. I let it ding into voice mail, then check it. It's Ammi, sobbing. "I'm so sorry, Rania. This wasn't supposed to happen. We'll get you out. I promise. I have to go, beta. This isn't my phone. I love you both." It's like everything I've ever understood about us, our situation, has widened into this huge movie screen. It's not just me and Kamal. Or Ammi in Pennsylvania. Something bigger is going on: the white tents we've seen on the news; the shifting lines; the children sleeping curled on concrete floors; and now here, covering their faces. We are disappearing, into the holes and crevices of this country.

— — —

"You straighten everything out?"

It's the next day, and I look up from our table to see that boy—Carlos, the one who draws. He carries around a battered army backpack with a beige sketchbook sticking out of the flap. We're eating lunch, though Kamal is mostly picking at his peanut butter and jelly sandwich.

I want to inch away, so I don't have to see him gloat, but he plops down beside me, straddling the bench. "It's just a matter of time. I've got connections," I tell him.

He gives me a skeptical grin.

"What? You don't believe me?"

"Connections," he says softly.

"Yes! My best friend! She's taking care of it."

His face goes quiet. "That's great, then. You can say goodbye to this five-star hotel."

He taps the table and gently ruffles Kamal's hair. "In the

meantime, hermanito, you want to play soccer with me?" He lifts up a ball, spinning it in his palm.

Kamal looks up from his moping. He's as sad as I am—missing Ammi, his last day of classes, playing with Derek and Amir.

"Go ahead, Kamal." I check my phone. It's been a whole day and Fatima still hasn't called or texted. "Thanks," I add.

Carlos bows, making me flush. "My pleasure."

I watch them melt into the haze of the courtyard, join the other boys. This Carlos kid is so annoying. But I'm grateful he took Kamal to play. Last night I stretched out beside my brother, his head cradled under my arm until his breaths went even and he fell asleep. He's back to chewing on his collar and last night I had to strip his bed and do an extra wash. Sometimes I think that is why Kamal is so quiet. He was born out of terror and flight. A boy who carries all our secrets, what came before.

Now I hear someone shout, "Goal!" Kamal's arms are thrust up in the air. The kids are crammed into a tight circle, shouting, "Game! Game!" Carlos winks, gives me a thumbs-up. I swivel away, trying to ignore the airy lift in my heart.

— — —

I don't know how he does it, but Carlos has a way of charming everyone—the social workers, the kids, the men who push mops across the floor. He draws Rosa and she is always pleased. One morning she wears a shirt with a bear that has sewn-on jiggly buttons for eyes. When we're clearing our trays, I give her a teasing poke in the stomach and she lets out a laugh. It's the most I've heard from her, and I find myself suddenly buoyed and laughing too.

After meals, Carlos always plays soccer with Kamal in the courtyard. It's not long before a cluster of boys gather around Carlos and they zigzag in the tight space. He does this again after dinner, which is my favorite time of day, when the heat seeps away from the concrete yard. I'll bring some novel from the rec room, or scribble in my notebook, while watching them play. I notice Carlos toss back his hair, showing that streak of bad dye. Still, he always makes sure to kick the ball to Kamal, who is shy, and easily winds up chasing after the pack. Sitting on the steps, in the dwindling light, you can't tell we're locked in: The kids are just shapes, moving, free.

"Why do you keep following me?" I ask.

He chuckles. "Look around, you see anyone else our age?"

It's true; most of the kids here are pretty young.

"When's your birthday?" I ask.

"October. I hit eighteen and adios! Deportado." He makes a swooping motion with his hand.

"How can you joke about it?"

"What do you want me to do? Cry all the time?"

"What about yelling?"

He pats his knees, stands. "I leave that to you, amiga."

Amiga. Friend. He's not my friend, I tell myself. Fatima is. But she still hasn't gotten back to me about the guardianship paper. *Hold tight,* she keeps texting. Lidia has texted too, told me she's working on my mother's release but she doesn't have much more to report.

"So, why are you here?" I ask him.

He hesitates a moment, as if deciding whether to tell me. Then he sits back down on the bench. "I was living with my aunt in Long Island." He starts rubbing his palms on his jeans knees, back and forth. "There was a raid at the factory where she worked." He pauses. "She did everything for me. She got me here. She bought me this art stuff. She didn't care. Just as long as I stayed out of trouble."

"What kind of trouble?"

"You don't want to know." He glances away. I notice two faint scars, like thin lightning, streaking his neck.

"Have you always drawn like that?" I ask, pointing to his backpack.

"Yeah. I used to do pictures for the tourists. In Guanajuato. One day this guy saw me draw and he offered to pay for my school. A better school. It was weird. He didn't have any kids of his own. So I got to go to a school where I learned English. Everything was going great but then he died. And his family didn't want to keep paying. That's when my aunt sent for me. I was lucky."

That word again. *Lucky.* Different. Special. But those aren't my words. They were my mother's. And they aren't helping me anymore.

— — —

Five days here. Five days to graduation.

Soon Carlos and I start finding each other at different times, pretending it's by chance. After the little kids' naptime. Lunch, when he slips us some chocolate bars. Or down in the basement, where there's a pool table and he practices tilting the cue stick from behind his back. Carlos is kind of a Peter Pan— the little kids just flock to him, like pigeons, cooing, nudging, and begging him to play. I start sneaking looks at Carlos—his slim hips, the way he runs in the courtyard, kicking the ball, calling to the kids, sliding in and out of Spanish. There's a tickling warmth in my ribs.

"Good evening, madam," he greets me, sitting down and setting the soccer ball between his feet. Sweat glosses his collarbone.

"Why 'madam'?"

"You're fierce. Scary. Like my teachers. My physics teacher, man, she was the worst."

"I'm not that scary," I say.

He grins. "Good to know."

"Wait. When did you get here?"

"A few weeks before you."

"You don't get to walk at graduation either?"

"Amiga, that ship sailed." His face looks suddenly tired, old, and he thrusts up from the step and walks away.

In the courtyard, I spot a group of the boys, standing in a knot in a corner, laughing loudly. Several of them are pinching their noses and pointing. Pushing through, I find Kamal hunched on the ground, his arms wrapped around his knees. His cheeks are streaked gray with tears.

"What's going on here?"

The boys just giggle; most of them only speak Spanish.

"Tell me!" I demand.

"Stink." A boy pinches his nose. "Stinky."

I grab Kamal by the wrist and yank him away. Upstairs I

make him strip off his clothes and then drag him into the shared bathroom, locking the door, and blast the shower. He's sobbing. I'm furious at those boys, but at Kamal too, for being able to make a mess and cry when all I get to do is stuff my fear down and worry.

"It's too hot!" he shrieks, but I grab him by the arm and force him under the streaming water. I scrub his slick body, then rub, hard with a washcloth, and he wails, "Rania, stop, you're hurting!" But I cannot stop. Finally, he goes still and I do too, hating him, hating myself, and all we are becoming.

— — —

The next morning Rosa isn't at our table. I ask Carlos, who keeps staring down at his drawing pad on his knees. "She has her hearing," he finally says.

"I don't understand."

"Don't you get it? They put her up there. In front of some kind of immigration judge. She's lucky because the shelter got her a lawyer."

"By herself?"

"Yup." He bites the word off, bitter.

"But she doesn't talk!"

"Exactly."

He unwinds his long legs and leaves.

I find him later, in a stairwell. He's sitting with his wrists on his knees, breathing hard. Now I see there are two Carloses: the charming one who kicks a soccer ball and gives out chocolate bars. And this one, his voice tight with grief. We start to talk—slowly—and he tells me about his own journey here, after his aunt sent for him. There were the trains and the coyote he met at a border town. The days that were so hot his belt buckle singed his fingers; the freezing nights, scrabbling over hard ground, overhead the stars like flashing knives. Once he crouched next to a pile of old bones bleached from the desert sun—those who'd crossed and didn't make it.

"Why did you leave?" I ask.

"After I lost my patron I went to a different school, where there were boys who picked on me. Then these other guys beat them up. They told me they wanted me to join them. A gang." He takes a while before he speaks again. "I kept saying no. I tried to do like before. I would go and draw the tourists that came in the main square. But one night I was followed. They took everything—my pencils and they slashed up my drawings. They said they needed me because my English was good, and next time it would be worse. I didn't believe them. I thought they were just big-mouth boys throwing their weight around. I went to the place where I buy my supplies. A little shop. The owner sometimes gave me things on credit. And I guess . . ." Here he falters.

"Carlos?"

"They found him. He was hurt bad. He went to the hospital." He adds, "It was all my fault."

He rubs the inside of his arm. "My aunt sent me the money and I ran away. And when I finally got here, I had the tattoo done. It's me as two fishes, swimming away. You can see the bones inside too. The bones I saw in the desert."

I watch his chest draw inward, as if gathering all his strength.

"You wouldn't believe it, but when we moved from Connecticut to Long Island a few months ago, at the high school, they thought my tattoo meant I was part of a gang. So stupid. Like the guys I'm running from! They sent some policeman to talk to me." He adds, "I feel like I'm always running."

We both go quiet. I feel a small pulse of recognition, remembering our suitcase, always packed in the closet. Carlos's lips are beautiful, curved. But his eyes are sad, so sad. We keep a space between us, almost because touching might hurt too much.

"Me too," I finally say.

— — —

Late afternoon: a group of kids having fun at a table, collaging keepsake boxes with shiny squares and stars and glue. I put a star on Kamal's nose and he squeals with laughter. Then my phone buzzes. I almost don't pick up, but then I see it's Fatima. She's crying. "I hate him!" she says.

"Who?"

"My father! He said no! He doesn't want my mom getting involved."

I lean back against my chair, take a few sharp breaths.

"I'm so sorry," she cries. "I begged my mom. To please, not to listen to him. For once!" She sniffles. "But she would never do that. God, how I hate them both."

I don't have time to hate either of them.

I wrench up from the table, out of the room and up the stairs, just as Carlos comes bounding toward me, proudly flourishing a cinnamon bun in a wrapper, dripping with icing. I try to push past him, but he blocks me. His face goes still. "Someone disappoint you?"

My throat constricts. "How did you know?"

"I know what it's like," he says softly.

"I just want to go to graduation! Sleep in my own bed." I drop down on a step, tears welling in my eyes.

He looks awkward, arms dangling, then sits beside me. "That's the worst thing. Figuring out who you can count on."

"She was my best friend," I whisper.

"Maybe she still is."

He hands me the cinnamon roll. I take a bite. The icing melts sweet in my mouth.

— — —

That night, like all nights, is the hardest. The cries that pierce the dark. There's an air conditioner in our window but even with the gurgling hum, still I can hear them: the shuffling, restless sounds of other children. Lost children. I keep seeing the desert that Carlos described: a terrible dry field, riven with cracks and fissures. Too many sounds: those who call out in terror. Or the ones who whimper. The others like Rosa who are numb and shiny-eyed, mute. Which is worse. I see all the faces of the social workers, drawn and tired; the art therapist who keeps coaxing children to draw what they feel. I climb up the bunk ladder and gaze at Kamal, stroking his hair. I just want to look and touch him, over and over.

He rolls over, mumbling, "What?"

"Nothing," I say.

Hours tick by. Graduation in three days. Instagram's blown up with my friends at school. A party in Prospect Park. Another in someone's basement. Fatima's selling braided hair ties with the school colors—purple and white. But it's Senior Day at Coney Island that most gets me. I play that post over and over: Fatima dancing on the sand, blowing kisses. Her curly hair bounces. Her shoulders are bare and tanned, which must have freaked her mother out. Her whole face shines, like a lit-up sun. Everyone celebrating—without me. I dream about the desert, about glittering stars and bones.

I've disappeared.

Chapter Nine

"You okay?"

It's lunch and Carlos is leaning across the table, his sketch pad put to the side. "After what happened with your friend. And I heard you the other day, when the kids made fun of Kamal. I was passing by the bathroom."

There's a stinging sensation around my ears, like when I get a sunburn at the beach. I don't like the idea of him knowing all my personal business. "And?" I ask.

"He's just a kid."

"Thanks for the news flash."

"Oh boy. Madam has returned."

"Can we drop it?"

Carlos doesn't say anything but picks up his spoon. We have chocolate pudding today for dessert but it looks too gelatinous, too shiny for me. I'm tired of eating food that tastes bland and slippery. I just want to go back to the apartment, slip into my own bed, and fry eggs for Kamal. Every day we stay here it's like another part of me blurs.

"So, what's the plan?" Carlos asks.

Even though Carlos and I sat in the stairwell and he told

me his terrible story, I don't want to talk. "What are you, my caseworker?"

He grins, sucking in some of that disgusting pudding. "You told me it's a mistake you're here. So how are you going to fix it?"

"Go yell at Ms. Kaplan again. For the millionth time."

He shakes his head. "That won't work. My aunt used to say: *The bull doesn't get what he wants. The cat does.*"

I sigh. "What kills me is graduation. I just want to go."

"So we have to do something."

"We?" I give him a smirk-smile.

He nods, smiling. "Why not?"

"I really need to find my uncle."

"There you go."

"What do you mean?"

He moves closer. My chest pumps wildly. Is he going to kiss me? Instead, he stands from the table, pulls his jeans up around his slim hips, smooths down his black hair. "Watch me."

— — —

An hour later, Carlos told me to follow him as he strides into Ms. Kaplan's office, holding up a bakery box and a large coffee. "Hola, Ms. Kaplan. Look what I've brought you!" He flips open the top with flair, showing four plump jelly doughnuts. He'd gotten one of the kitchen staff to run down the block to get them—he made friends with her since she's from his hometown. He sets down the coffee. "See, I got it just the way you like it. With skim milk."

Ms. Kaplan looks up tiredly. "Carlos, what is it now?"

He pats me on the shoulder. "Look, Rania is an amazing student. She's getting an award. Can't you let her go to graduation?"

"No can do. I don't have any staff to take her. Two of my vans are out for repair."

Carlos beams. "Then I can be her escort. You can trust me. I will bring her back, one, two, three, quick."

She laughs. "Carlos, you can't be the escort!" But she does snap off the container lid and gratefully sip the coffee. "Let me see if I can find someone from another one of our facilities to take her."

"And me!"

She tilts her head, laughing again. Carlos seems to find ways to move around the rules. But I don't trust him completely. Even when he looks away for a second I see a sadness in his face. He's got secrets tucked away, his eyes on the present.

But even Carlos can't charm us out of here: a little while later, we're in the rec room, and Ms. K pulls me aside and says she just couldn't find anyone to take me to graduation. "I'm so sorry, Rania."

I leap up from the sofa, rush into the corridor, kick a wall until I can't anymore.

— — —

A brush against my arm. I look up to see Carlos, putting a finger to his lips, motioning me away. We go down a few halls, through the kitchen, where a cook grins at him and calls out in Spanish, and then out into the alley. There he shows me the fence and a broken lock. "This is how we get to your graduation."

"This is nuts!"

"We'll leave early, before the morning shift. Just take a few things."

"What about Kamal?"

"Can he stay quiet?"

"Too quiet."

I shift on my feet, uneasy. I've never done anything like this. But something in me doesn't care. I have to get out of here. Go to graduation. "What about after?" I ask. "I can't come back here."

"You still want to find your uncle?"

I nod.

"That too. We'll find him."

— — —

Early hours: gray on gray, blinds drawn, the room quiet. I pack up our belongings, just enough, stuffing a change of clothes, my laptop and phone, my cap and gown into my backpack; some items for Kamal in his bag. I tap Kamal awake and he quietly climbs down the ladder and follows me downstairs. I told him how we were going on a fun trip, first to my graduation, then somewhere special.

The halls are dim, but we find our way through the kitchen. Out the back, through the courtyard and into the alley. The lock is still broken, just the way Carlos said. I tug it loose, step out onto the pavement. It's still early; the streets are mostly empty.

Stomach clenched, I glance behind me. Where's Carlos? Maybe I was stupid to ever agree to this plan.

A door snaps open, footsteps. I spin around. It's Carlos, running, his backpack hiked over his shoulder, his sketchbook jutting out over the flap.

"What happened to you?"

"Sorry. I couldn't find my pencils."

I start to walk away. "Great. My graduation and you have to worry about some pencils."

"Rania, wait!"

"What?" I swerve around. He looks genuinely sorry.

"It's just . . . I can't go anywhere without my drawing stuff."

Now it's me who feels sorry. "My bad," I whisper.

Then Kamal starts jumping up and down, the straps of his backpack squeaking on his shoulders. "Please, Carlos!" he begs. "Come with us! It'll be so much fun!"

My eyes swing to the corner. The subway is three blocks away. "Hurry," I say.

— — —

Carlos is right on this front too: going to graduation, even sneaking out, is worth it. My class, sitting crammed in the hot auditorium, silky nylon sleeves floating around our arms, sticking to our bare legs. There's a flutter of a thousand programs, since everyone is using them as fans. I look over the sea of heads and spot Kamal, beaming at me. Carlos sits where Ammi should be. I gulp down the hurt in my throat. Then my name is called for my award, and I struggle across the stage, sandal straps digging into my toes. Ms. Ricardo gives me a hug. "Good luck, Rania," she says, and

I realize she knows nothing of what's happened to me. I'm just another senior who flaked out in the last days.

After the ceremony, we mill on the grass, clutching our diplomas, limp gowns clinging to our damp arms, our necks. A few people toss their caps and I watch the mortarboards angle up into the air. I hug Ginny and Sylvia and Layla—the crew Fatima and I sometimes hung with. But my eyes well with tears, seeing all the parents and grandparents embracing, their arms teeming with flowers. Fatima is surrounded by her brothers and cousins, Mrs. Elawady looking happy but distracted, Mo tugging on her arm. Mr. Elawady is avoiding me. Fatima's eyes meet mine; she rushes over and throws her arms around me. "I can't believe you made it!"

"Shh." I draw near, put my mouth to her ear. "Pretend you didn't see me."

"But—"

"I have to go. I'll text you later."

She gives me an inquiring look, then regards Carlos. "Cute," she whispers. "Who is he?"

"A friend."

She turns to Carlos. "You take care of her, right?" She pulls me close, her long earrings dangling cool on my neck. "I love you," she whispers.

Then we are out of there, fast. We don't have much time.

— — —

The apartment smells stale. Nothing is wrong—Maria Auntie has clearly come in and watered the plants over the last ten days—

the spider leaves spring to my touch. She's thoughtfully put the mail on the front table and left a few notes where the car was last parked. The refrigerator has been emptied of perishables, plastic containers left to dry upside down in the rack.

Carlos helps Kamal pack more clothes and pick his toys, while I snap open my laptop, put in my mother's password, and pay off the utilities and the rent and a few small bills. Then I pull belongings from the closet—Carlos finds me, sitting cross-legged, stuck, staring bleakly.

"Hey," he says and kneels down beside me. "You okay?"

"I guess." I look at him. "What about you? What are you going to do?"

He shrugs. "I can't stay there. In a few months, when I'm eighteen, they'll send me back."

"Can't you ask your lawyer?"

He shakes his head. "I don't have a lawyer, Rania. I don't have the money."

"Don't you have a plan? I mean, you can't just run forever!"

He looks sad. "Sometimes that's all you can do."

I wish I hadn't been so mean, so quick-tempered. And Carlos is right. Sometimes running is all we can do. Isn't that what Ammi taught me? "Sorry," I mumble, and he goes to help Kamal pack.

My cell dings with a text from Lidia: *Rania, Where r u??? Call me ASAP.*

Quickly, I pull out the orange vinyl bag from the back. As I'm taking the manila folder, my hand brushes against what feel like lumps of candy in a zippered compartment. Inside I find a velvet string bag. When I spill the contents onto the floor, there it is: a gold and pearl and ruby-studded choker. Earrings. Bangles. I had forgotten what Ammi told me: Find the jewelry. Sell it for a good price.

Since when did my mother have such expensive things?

I twist from the floor, all of me electric, fearful.

"What's up?" Carlos stands in the hall, holding Kamal's duffel bag.

I stuff the choker back into its bag and shove it, along with the bangles, into a zippered compartment in my backpack.

"We have another stop."

— — —

Mr. Mehta's eyes glint with pleasure as he strokes the choker draped in his palm. "Very nice!" He wedges in his eyepiece to examine all the pieces, fingering every filigreed bit. "Your mother must have had a very big wedding."

"Not really. My parents were like—" I want to say: Activists. Students. Progressive. He's busy weighing the jewelry, punching at his calculator, then he swivels it around to show the number: fifteen hundred dollars. "Cash," he adds.

The floor seems to float under my feet, imagining all that money. Tucked in my bag are the bangles, just in case.

I agree, folding the bills into my wallet, then I watch him lift the jewelry, press a buzzer, and disappear into a back room. I feel a swipe of loss, for something I didn't even know was mine.

Connecticut

Chapter Ten

Okay, so this is about the dumbest thing I've ever done. Me, my little brother, and this guy Carlos on the road in search of some phantom uncle who will sign the form tucked in my backpack and save the day. Save us? What does that even mean? All I know is I can't go back to the shelter. I steer our car out of its parking spot, up Coney Island Avenue, toward the Brooklyn Queens Expressway ramp. Kamal's in the back, happily eating greasy pakoras he and Carlos bought while I went to the jewelers.

"We could pick up a few fares," Carlos jokes, pointing to my mom's decal.

"Yeah, right."

"You know, I got a license too," he says.

"How'd you get that?"

He smiles. "In Connecticut, where we lived before, it's not so hard to get one. Comes in handy, right?"

"Right," I say with a laugh. This Carlos guy thinks of everything.

According to my GPS, we should reach Stamford in an hour and a half. Carlos told me he's along for the ride and then he is going to figure out a way to get to Boston, where his aunt has a friend. He doesn't have an exact plan. He's just putting one foot in front of the other. What he really wants to do is go to art school. When he lived with his aunt, he used to spend whatever extra money he had on sketch pads and pencils, and after watching a YouTube video, he started taking the train into the city to wander around the Metropolitan Museum of Art. His aunt wasn't sure what to make of him but she was just glad he stayed out of trouble.

I haven't told Kamal where we're going, as I don't want to get his hopes up. About an hour after we've left the slow-moving Bronx traffic, we're turning into the exit for Stamford, and then driving under the highway, bumping down a narrow road. The address I have brings us to a development of low town houses, grouped in small clusters. As we park, I can see, behind a fence, a small swimming pool, and a marina, boats bobbing at the dock. It takes us a while to find the exact town house where Salim lives, but no one answers—the bell just booms and booms. I try to peek inside the slender window but I can't see much—what looks like an empty, long room.

"Hello?" A woman is coming toward us, dressed in a large straw hat, a thin cover-up, and flip-flops. It looks like she's coming from the pool.

I take a step back, nervous. "Does Salim live here?"

She tilts her head, showing a sunburnt face sprayed with freckles. "He moved. A few months ago."

"Do you know where he is?" I ask. Then I add, "I'm his niece."

"Oh. I didn't know he had any relatives here."

"We lost touch." I quickly add, "I've got some mail of his."

She hesitates, as if she's trying to figure out if this is true.

But she's friendly, chatty even. "He's not far away, about forty minutes. I guess after the business with RBS, they had to move." She sets down her straw bag and inserts her key in a door. "If you wait here, I can find the address he gave me." A few minutes later she returns with a scrap of paper. "I do miss them. The boy and girl were so cute." She smiles at Kamal. "You're going to see your cousins?"

Kamal's eyes widen.

When we get back in the car, he keeps asking, "Am I going to see my cousins?"

I wince. "I hope."

"When?"

"Soon."

"How many cousins do I have?"

"Two, I think. A boy and a girl."

"Are you sure?"

"I'm not sure."

"Is that where we're going?"

I swing the car out onto the road. "Yes," I say. "That's where we're going."

— — —

Family. Cousins. Why are these words so hard to say? Why do they always feel as if there's a serrated knife cutting through my chest, leaving a jagged trail of half memories? I remember once or twice visiting my grandparents. A large bungalow set behind a gate, where a driver was busy flicking a rag on their car. Inside a big garden, there were many children, and we played a game where we had to sit on balloons until they popped, but the noise scared me, so I ran and hid behind my mother's legs. "She's scared, not like you were, Sadia," someone said through laughter. I remember feeling angry but I didn't say anything because Ammi told me to be on my best behavior when we went to Nani and Nana's house. I only caught a glimpse of Nana—an older man at the end of a long corridor, with his hands cupped behind his back. He turned once, and I noticed the white brush of his mustache, his fierce eyes. He neither frowned nor smiled, but then turned back to his walking and disappeared into a room. Later someone told me he was watching us from behind the shutters but he never came out. I got drowsy from eating too many sweets and all I remember is being carried in my mother's arms into a taxi, and my nani, who visited us sometimes, kept insisting that she let the driver take us, but Ammi said no, a taxi was fine. I could hear the clash and hurt in their voices. It seemed it was always this way, even the few times Nani came to visit, carrying a big bag full of long beans and potatoes and onions. "We aren't starving!" Ammi would cry. "Naved makes a good salary."

My phone has gone haywire with messages, all from Ms. Kaplan. She's nervous, then angry, then furious. *This is not funny, Rania. Are you with Carlos? Do you know what kind of trouble we can get into?* I pull the car over and walk a few feet away to call Lidia, who picks up quickly, demanding, "Where are you?" I can hear honking in the background, the shuffling sound of her movement down a street.

"I'm on my way to my uncle's."

"Oh, Rania." There's disappointment in her voice.

"You said it! He can sign the paper, saying he's a standby guardian. And maybe he can help us—"

"They're frantic at the shelter!"

"Can you call them?"

I hear her sigh. "No, I can't."

"Please, Lidia. Just give me a little time. To find out more. About my uncle, about my—" I want to say family, but I bite the word off. I'm not sure what I'm looking for—answers, safety, a way to get my mother out of that gray detention center in Pennsylvania.

Another muddled sound as she moves the phone. "We can't be having this conversation, okay? I can't know anything. Not where you are. Not where you're going."

I swallow. "Okay." My voice has shrunk small.

"I'll have to tell your mother—"

"Wait. Please. Not yet."

A long silence. "One day," she says. "I'll give you one day." Then she clicks off.

When I return to the car, I try to put on a brave face. My whole body feels as if I've been rubbed hard with a washcloth; I am tingling, afraid. I've never done anything like this before. Maybe this is what my father used to feel, going on his assignments, chasing down a lead, a dangerous interview: dizzy-scared, but exhilarated too.

— — —

The street where Salim Uncle lives is sorry-looking: small boxy houses with worn-down metal fences. We pull up to a pale-green home with concrete steps, a tricycle turned on its side on the front lawn. A clothesline in the back, an orange shalwar fluttering in the breeze like a bright flag. The right place, I think.

Again I tell Carlos to wait with Kamal in the car, and make my way up the path and press the bell. When the door swings open, I'm facing a heavyset man who vaguely resembles Ammi, with thicker features. "May I help you?" he asks.

"I'm Rania," I blurt out, then add, "Your niece."

What was I thinking? That there would be bolts of lightning? A happy rainbow arcing over the backyard? Instead Salim Uncle looks confused. "Niece?" he repeats.

"Sadia's daughter. I . . . got your address from Hema Auntie. She gave me the old place and—"

"You are Rania?" he interrupts. "I haven't seen you since—" He puts a palm out to show a little child. I remember what Ammi said, *He is the soft-hearted one,* and for a brief moment I imagine a jolly man ready to scoop us up in his burly arms. Then he squints at Carlos, who's leaning against the hood, and Kamal, staring through the open window. "Who is this?"

I swallow. "That's Kamal. Your nephew."

"Nephew," he repeats softly.

"And . . . a friend."

Poor Salim Uncle! He looks befuddled, as if he's always in this disheveled state: wavy, unkempt hair, a wrinkled shirt over khaki pants, bare feet. I can see he's struggling to make sense of me, of this moment. He squints. "Your mother, where is she?"

I rock back on my heels. If I blurt out where she is, what we want, I'm afraid he'll just send us packing. Or will he? He's still, rubbing his jaw, as if recovering from the surprise. "It's compli- cated," I say.

He gives a wary bob of his head. "Chalo. Come in."

The house feels odd, in a state of disorder, like Uncle: suitcases are stacked in the hall and open boxes near the dining area, the walls stripped bare. He indicates the living room. "Please. Please sit down." Then he asks us to wait and he disappears upstairs.

I can hear two voices, low and whispering, with a few phrases popping out. *Typical,* I hear. *And this boy? Just like Sadia. We cannot have this now.* Carlos, who has sat opposite me, mouths, *Should I go?* but I shake my head. This doesn't feel like a family reunion at all.

A few minutes later a woman glides down the stairs. She is slender, her thick hair clipped back, her eyes heavily kohled, and she introduces herself as Shaima, Uncle's wife. She seems young, shy, but also intimidated, glancing at my uncle for guid- ance, then smiling broadly at Kamal. "Hello there! You wish to give Auntie a kiss?"

Kamal, who's been sitting quietly next to Carlos, obliges her, but he is stiff and awkward. "Uncle too," Shaima instructs, and Kamal does his duty, and then quickly scoots back to me, press- ing his head against my side. I stroke his hair. My stomach is hurting something awful. I don't know where to begin.

Fortunately, Shaima has gone into the kitchen to put on tea and keeps chattering about this and that—how empty her cup- boards, how the children are true power nappers, so it might be a while before they wake. Uncle is staring at Kamal and me, up and down, as if trying to place us. After Kamal crams his mouth with biscuits, she suggests he might want to play outside, where there's a swing set. I take this as a strong hint—Uncle and Auntie want to see me alone—and so Carlos takes him by the hand, through the sliders and outside. For a second, I wish I could join them, be a kid.

"So, Rania," Uncle begins. "You can imagine what a surprise this is. I have not spoken to your mother in a very long time. How is she?"

There's a raw roughness threatening to spill out of my eyes. "Not great." I add, "She's in detention."

"Detention?"

"I mean, immigration. There was this raid. Some kind of problem with our application—" And then I tell them in one long gulp: about the night the men came in their black vests; about my mother's asylum application, Mrs. Flannery and her mean eyes, and about Carlos who has been the only person to make me feel normal since this all started. I don't know why I tell them so much. It's not like me. I'm used to squeezing everything shut, tight, like a jar top. Just the way Ammi taught me. But there's something about sitting opposite these two who I am supposed to call Auntie and Uncle.

When I look up, they both are half-frozen, faces stricken. I wish I could stuff it all back inside, every one of my words.

— — —

I spend dinner snatching glances at Uncle: his thick wrists, his bushy eyebrows, looking for signs of Ammi and me. He is related, but there are holes, gaps. One part of me wants to yell, *Why don't you just help us? Why aren't you in touch with your own sister?* But I swallow the words down. I think of what Carlos said: *The bull doesn't get what they want. The cat does.* Carlos has endeared himself to everyone, making silly faces at Roshaan and Maira, who giggle and beg for more. I like him so much right now.

Shaima keeps apologizing for the state of the house. The packing is going slow, especially with two young ones—Roshaan and Maira, only a year apart. The boy is energetic, barreling through the house like a little linebacker—it's his tricycle in the front. Maira, who has her father's curly hair and wide, round face, keeps clinging to her mother's legs as she cooks. I feel a pang because I want to scoop her up into my lap, but I can't tell what's allowed.

"You're moving?" I ask.

"It appears so," Salim Uncle says with a sigh.

"We're returning to Lahore," Shaima puts in. "We'll stay with my parents."

"But I thought you lived here!" I bang down my fork.

Carlos, who has kept quiet the whole time, is appreciatively scooping up his food. Shaima is a good cook, unlike Ammi, who does it distractedly. He answered a few questions from Uncle, explained that he had taken the ride because he is on his way to a relative in Boston, that he hopes to live there and go to art school. We both know it's a lie. Or a half lie. We're running on faint vapors, fantasies of how to right this strange trip we're on.

"I was here on a work visa. Analytics for the bank. But the position I received was—"

"It was below your qualifications," Shaima snaps. "Back home—"

Uncle puts up a hand. "It's true. It wasn't what I expected. The place was very cut-throat. I expected something else."

Pride. This soft man—underneath he has the same stubborn, hard pride as Ammi.

"When it came time for my renewal after three years, usually a routine thing, my supervisor said they wouldn't be able to re-sponsor me. There were some problems. Word had come down that they needed to hire an American. Even though I'd built up the whole department."

I remember Lidia's office, the phones ringing off the hook, the noise of so many people, their lives abruptly put in limbo.

"We waited awhile, thinking the situation would resolve it-self. But the way things are going in this country—"

"Salim," Shaima warns. Clearly the talk is usually much sharper, more bitter.

"We decided we might as well leave."

The children are restless, so we clear the table, load the dish-washer, and push open the sliders so Uncle and I sit out on the patio. Shaima has disappeared to do a load of laundry. It's early evening and the tree leaves are lit up like bits of gold foil. Carlos has taken over with the kids, just the way he did at the shelter, letting them chase him around the yard. Whoops of laughter spin in the air. The neighbors are barbecuing and the smell of charred meat drifts over. I watch them in a blur of sadness. This scene seems so soft, so normal, and I ache to just remain here, to never leave.

With my heart beating wildly in my chest, I start. "You

see, Uncle, with Ammi in detention, we need someone to sign for us."

"Sign?"

"It's a form." I twist around and pull it from my backpack. "You can say you'll be in charge of us." I'm still holding the folded paper, between us, so I add, "You don't really have to. It's just a signature. We'll go back to the apartment, wait for Ammi to get out. Lidia says it will happen. Any day now."

Uncle does not say anything, but gazes off at the children streaking across the yard, squealing with laughter as Carlos flings himself down on the grass. They are clambering on top of him—his stomach, his legs, even his face, and he doesn't seem to mind. Then I see the sad shadows on Uncle's face. My heart is breaking. Because I can tell: he is going to say no. This was why it was so hard to bring up my request. I didn't want to know. I didn't want to come right up against his back, turning away from me. Exactly what Ammi used to say: *They turned against me, Rania. All of them.*

"Is it because of my grandfather?"

Uncle looks puzzled.

"Nana," I continue. "He was so mean to Ammi."

He sighs. Then he takes the form, looks down at it for a bit. "Rania," he says. "I wish I could. But if I sign this, there might be problems. My own immigration. We leave in two weeks. And—"

Here he hesitates. The darkness is full-on, like a curtain that has come draping down, embroidered with the checkered windows of the other houses. There's grit under my lids. Why, I think, is this so hard—something as simple as family?

"Rania . . . child. You are so lovely. So intelligent. Of course Sadia would bring such a girl into the world."

The grit is thick on my lashes, so I see everything through wet clumps.

"It is best that the rest of the family doesn't learn that I have seen you."

"But why?"

"It is for your own good."

"My own good!"

"If your father would know—"

I gasp. It's as if the air had turned solid, slammed into me. I start to shake. Abu—alive? A flood of memories rush up, hurtling against me: Abu, leaning over me as I'm curled in bed. Abu at the table, correcting my spelling—he was as strict as Ammi. Abu, beneath a blue cloud of cigarette smoke on the balcony, then rushing away after a phone call came in. I've stuffed it all into that lockbox of memories, a time that can't exist.

Then I look at Uncle. He seems crushed, his shoulders bowed.

"What do you mean?" I ask. I can hardly breathe. "My father?"

Chapter Eleven

Ammi loves houses.

Sunday mornings I'd hear the jangle of keys and I'd wake to see her standing over me, her freshly showered hair pinned up with a clip. "Come," she'd say. "We're going to see some listings." I'd groan but she was already bustling around the apartment, stuffing her notebook into her big bag, filling a thermos with coffee, packing bags of nuts and sandwiches, and pushing us out the door for open houses.

In the beginning we'd look at places in the boroughs—sometimes, abandoned skinny houses in the farthest reaches of Brooklyn, their aluminum siding falling off, concrete stoops broken, garbage overflowing in the cans. Another time, a two-family in Queens with a carved aluminum gate and a satellite dish on the roof, where she wound up chatting in Urdu with a neighbor who told her about the family that was selling. Now and then, we'd do a fancy brownstone neighborhood and we'd have to wait behind people who filed up the stoop. Once inside, eyes shining, Ammi would admire the sleek kitchens and bleached wood floors; the carved pier mirror where someone had hung one hat, just so; the tasteful bedrooms with sun streaming through folded back shutters.

"What do you think, Rania?" she'd ask.

"It's okay." I knew we couldn't afford any of it.

Ammi always told me how much they're worth—That one's three mil, she'd say. And look at that one. It's got two rentals so they'd clear nine thousand easy, that covers a lot of your mortgage. Though Sunset Park you can get one for a million and a half. That's where the white people are coming, so it's a better investment.

"A two-family," she'd murmur. "Yes, that's the way to go."

"Uh-huh," I'd mumble.

Sometimes I think that's what frustrated Ammi the most: that she couldn't get a hold of something and make it grow. There was a time when she signed on to an herbal supplement scheme—bottles and bottles were stacked up in our closet while she tried to sell it to everyone we knew. In the end she was out several hundred dollars, and Kamal and I had to go without new sneakers for a season. But then she was on to the next idea—Uber, while studying to be a real estate agent.

When I think of those Sundays, when we'd return, to our neighborhood, our building, with its scrappy garden in the front, and our little apartment, where the hallway smells and the bulbs blink over the bathroom sink—maybe we weren't running toward her dream but also away from something I have yet to figure out.

— — —

Salim Uncle is kind. Once the children are put to bed and we have figured out the sleeping arrangements—Kamal will sleep in

Maira and Roshaan's room, Carlos on the living room sofa—he takes me into a small room off the kitchen, his office. It too is filled with boxes—all that's left is a black desk and big vinyl chair, his computer, and a couch where I'll spend the night. I sit on the edge, still trembling, shock coiling through me.

"I am so sorry, Rania, that I am the one to tell you."

He drops into his chair and shifts toward me, hands bunched between his knees. Now I see: What I took for rumpled disarray is someone confused by emotion, easily tugged by others.

"Your mother was married young," he begins.

"To Abu?"

"No. Fawad."

I look at him, confused, before he continues.

"The families have known each other a long while. Fawad had been abroad to study, then Dubai, then back again. Sadia had everything—a big bungalow. Servants. A good life."

"A good life," I repeat faintly. What does this have to do with Abu?

"I was younger so I don't remember much of it, mind you. But people tell me Fawad changed. He was legendary—quite the party animal. He'd be the last on the dance floor. He wanted to be a rock musician! He sent away for all kinds of expensive electric guitars. After he married, though, he became more"—he seems to be groping for the word—"conservative."

"In what way?"

"I'd hear Sadia complaining to our mother. She said Fawad was so controlling. She couldn't even go out for lunch with her girlfriends without him badgering her. And the thing that most broke her heart was her studies."

"Ammi always said she stopped because I was born."

"There had been the agreement. Even if she married, she could keep studying. She had no lack of help! But Fawad began to pressure her. He didn't like her out by herself or with her friends from university. He hated that she'd joined the drama club, the debate club. He didn't think the house was being run properly."

"Did he hurt her?"

"No. He is not like that. But he is intimidating. He is the sort of person who corners you in a room, and if he sets on an idea, he won't let up. He makes you think as he does."

"I can't imagine Ammi putting up with that!"

"That's exactly it. That's why he chose her. He liked her spark. Her determination. He used to laugh and say they were a pair from *Taming of the Shrew,* only there was no taming her! He said of all the girls he knew, Sadia was an original. Until . . ." He hesitates.

"Until what?"

"Until Naved."

Up to this point I've been poised on the cushions, straining to take in every word that Uncle lays before me, hoping to hear more about Abu. But I sit back. It's as if faint smudges were becoming clearer. Ammi's obsessions with houses and real estate. *Let's live in that place where there's no one, let's go.* The way she breathed down my neck around my studies, my clubs. I sometimes felt it was as if she was trying to restore a place that already existed in her mind. As if she wanted me to grasp that she hadn't always slept on a foldaway couch, that she'd led a better, more exalted life.

"The thing of it is," Uncle continues, "my sister was very dramatic about it all. She flaunted her connection to Naved. Said she felt she'd met her true match. Her destiny. They were soul and body, a higher love."

I think of the ghazals Ammi loved to hum.

Piyaa baaj pyaala piyaa jaaye naa
Piyaa baaj jek til jiyaa jaaye naa

I can't ever drink my drink without my love
I can't ever breathe; I sink without my love

Be careful, she would tell me. *Always wait for the true one.*

"It was a mess," he continues.

"You're blaming my mother?"

"No, no, sweetie. But emotions ran high. Our father was angry. You can imagine the shame for our family. To have your daughter run away like that. To a penniless student! A journalist! With a small baby!"

I start. "Baby?"

Uncle's eyes look even more deep-set, ringed by crinkly half-moons. "Yes," he says quietly. "You were maybe six, seven months."

We go silent. The room seems to be an amusement park ride, shaking and blurring before me. So Abu is still gone. I'm not sure where I am. Who I am. "Did I know"—I cannot say the word *father*—"Ammi's first husband?"

He gives a helpless shrug. "They made an arrangement.

Everyone was so stubborn. Everyone took sides. Fawad, he was forced to accept your mother's choice, but it ate away at him all those years. And when Naved disappeared, the whole thing blew up."

"How?"

"Fawad had given your mother permission to take you to the conference in New York. But when she fled for good—"

"We had to! My father—"

"Naved was not your father."

"Yes, he is! He *was*!" Heat springs out of me, and then shame that he should know so much about me: that my mother never told me the truth, and some shadow man could have a claim on me. How dare he take away Abu, my abu, who used to carry me bouncing on his shoulders, who showed me how to swim in a pool and be fearless.

Uncle frowns. "You sound just like Sadia. Stubborn. The same as when I came here. Sadia was already demanding."

I stiffen. "Mona said Ammi wouldn't talk to you."

He sighs. "Not exactly. I knew a bit about the trouble your mother and Naved faced. And I knew, of course, about the family situation. She asked me to write something up for her application. When I said I could not, she was furious at me, told me no one had ever protected her."

"No one did." I remember lying in the hotel with Ammi, the scary men that seemed to crawl inside the walls.

His voice strains. "I suppose I was not a very good brother."

Then be one now, I want to say. But I bite down on my words. My hold on him, on family, is so tentative. I don't want to upset the balance.

"You have to understand, Rania, I had my own troubles. That's why I could not get involved. And Fawad is not a man to be . . . crossed." There's a chill on that word.

He stands, lets his hand rest on my shoulder. "Come, sweetie. It's time for rest."

— — —

Uncle goes out of the room, leaving me raw, stunned. I wait for everything to go still, for the shock to stop tumbling through me.

There's a plastic truck jammed into the pillow and I take it out, fiddling with its wheels. I stare at my phone, wishing I could just ring Ammi. *Why couldn't you tell me?* I search my memory for anyone who might be Fawad. Did I meet him the few times I went to my grandparents'? Does he know anything about me? How I loved my Dora the Explorer backpack, how I liked to write and make poems? I stretch my arms in front of me, then straighten my legs. Everyone always said I was tall but I thought it was because I took after Naved. Is Fawad tall too? I take out my phone, tempted to even search him down and then I realize I don't even know his last name. I have Abu's name. I scrunch these thoughts down. Who cares about some strange man? Several times I try to text Fatima, then delete my message. What am I supposed to say? *You thought your family was weird.*

Shaima slips in, carrying a sheet, a folded blanket, and a pillow. She's changed into a faded cotton print housedress and clipped up her hair, making her look even younger, barely a few years older than me. After tucking the sheet around the sofa

123

cushions, she straightens. "I'm so sorry, Rania. That was quite a lot to take in, wasn't it?"

"Yes," I say dully.

She pats the pillow. "Get some sleep, then."

I'm still rigid, unable to move.

"If it helps," she says, "I met Naved once. I see why your mother did what she did." Then she disappears through the doorway.

--- --- ---

Morning arrives, the sunshine astringent and clear. I did not sleep much last night. Snatches of memory: a younger uncle, chasing us around a garden. My grandmother giving me a sweet in a folded napkin. "Your ammi brings so much trouble," she whispered. *Trouble.* That word. Abu back home, in the dim room on the bed, legs drawn in. I went to hug him, but there was a big bandage around his head. He gave me a groggy smile. Other words, behind the shut door: *Abduction. Goons.* My stomach hurt. Ammi, nervous when we went to the market. The two of them arguing. *How long can we do this?* Ammi straightening my leather book bag on my shoulder, saying *Do not tell anyone at school.* That's when I began screwing everything shut inside me. Forgetting.

Now, as I get dressed, my thoughts are crisp, firm.

In the living room, I find Carlos sleeping with his wrist over his eyes. Leaning over, I whisper in his ear. He stirs, then springs up, heads for the bathroom, changes, and stuffs his dirty clothes in his backpack.

Shaima and I make breakfast together—eggs and buttered toast and instant coffee. I notice lines etched around the corners of her mouth, pulling them down; the tired blots of her eyes, just like Uncle's. It must have been lonely here for her, like my mother. And then I resent knowing this about the adults, their problems. Just a few weeks ago I was thinking about our graduation party on Rockaway Beach, and the summer, when I was going to stretch out under the gurgling air conditioner and read and train to work at a cute little bookstore.

"You could stay for a few days," she suggests. "There's a park where I take the children. It has a pool and is lovely."

"Thank you, Auntie. I should get back," I say, but the wish to linger wisps through me.

I let Kamal play with his cousins on the patio for a short bit while we have Nescafé and finish our toast. That's the only moment when I waver, unsure about what I'm doing. Then I work up my nerve and pull Uncle aside into the study, fishing out the standby guardian form. "Please sign it," I say.

He frowns. "Not possible."

"No one will know. We're just waiting for Ammi to get out."

"This is just like your mother! Arriving out of the blue, with a strange boy! No chaperone! Shaming our family all over again!" He makes a noise of disgust.

I wait for the anger to pass. "Please, Uncle," I say quietly. "Be a brother."

Uncle struggles to calm himself. "All right." He snatches the paper, swipes his pen across the signature line.

They wave to us on those crumbling steps, all four of them like a photo of a perfect family, the family I thought I wanted.

Uncle slipped some folded cash into my palm, insisting, "Take it," along with a slip of paper. "My mobile number and email. In case you need it."

I fold it into my pocket, look away.

"I am sorry, Rania. This country, it makes it so hard to be a family." He sets his palm against mine and it feels warm, heavy. "Inshallah. Maybe someday it will happen."

As I walk down the path, my vision is thick with tears.

In the car, Carlos looks at me. "Where to?"

I stare at my own hands on the wheel. They seem strange, as if they aren't a part of me. Then I see Carlos's lean profile, my backpack slumped at his feet with the form inside. Kamal, grinning in the back seat.

"Wherever you want," I say with a smile.

IV

On the Road

Chapter Twelve

We drive and drive, new ideas of where we'll go piling up, like fluffy clouds on the horizon. It's the last week of June, so why not treat it like a vacation? The aquarium. Fenway Park. Carlos keeps checking his phone and looking up places to see. "There's good pizza in Providence," he'll say, with a glance toward the back seat. Or "Maybe we should check out Legoland."

"Legoland!" Kamal chimes.

I don't know what I want to do, I just need to keep going. I don't want to be reminded of who I was: that girl in her army jacket and black boots, so sure of herself, of her past and future. That's the old Rania, like a deflated parade float, left on the pavement in a puddle of flattened rubber.

Everything a lie. This country a lie. Lidia's right: In fifth grade we went to Ellis Island. I wore my hair in braided loops in those days. I was still only a year into this country and I was eager and everything excited me—the ferry we took, the nice teachers, the buttons we could press lighting up the big map where everyone came from, the echoing halls where they waited. I wrote a report about a girl like me who came with her parents and whose luggage with torn straps I saw on display. Now every house we skim past seems made of paper, transparent, ready to blow over. But I do have Kamal in the back, Carlos beside me.

Since we don't have much in the way of clothes, we pull off when we see a mall and shop at TJ Maxx. I buy underwear, shorts, and a new pair of sneakers for Kamal, flip-flops and a straw hat for me. Carlos gets sunglasses and joggers, snapping off the labels as we walk back through the parking lot.

By late afternoon, we're searching for a motel just outside Boston. At the first one I snap down my driver's license, and the receptionist explains, "You can't book a room because you're under eighteen."

I gulp. That again. We turn away when an elderly man, reading in a chair, gestures to us. "Up the road," he says. "Pay cash."

We drive a short way to find a low-slung, dirty-yellow motel, its sign missing letters, so it says, OTEL. ACANCIES.

"'Ello, you have 'ooms at the 'otel?" Carlos teases as we walk toward the front door.

Kamal giggles and they start a chiming game, leaving off the first letters.

The shower curtain shrieks on its metal loops, showing a permanently stained tub. Our room looks out on a pool drained of water and a DO NOT USE sign. We don't care. We flop on the beds, arms out. The hours spread before us, delicious. No grownups. No one else. That's all I want right now. To not think or worry or be angry or scared.

Carlos pushes back a strand of hair that's fallen in front of my eyes. "You okay with all of this?" he asks.

I blush. "I think."

We both jump up, suddenly awkward. He's blushing too. The two double beds suddenly look different.

"Maybe we should wash up before dinner," I suggest.

"Good idea."

Our elbows bang. He springs back, gestures to the bathroom door. "You first." Then he steps outside, sketchbook tucked under his arm.

Polite, I think, unzipping my bag. Ammi would approve.

We all wash and change, then cross the busy road and eat at a Houlihan's, stuffing ourselves with fries and steak and chocolate cake. Groaning, we make our way back across, pausing on the meridian as the cars zip and hum past. I grab Kamal's hand, tugging him closer to me, and hold Carlos's arm, as if to brace myself against all this change and commotion.

"You okay?" Carlos asks.

A little jump in my throat, seeing his beautiful mouth, his eyes. In a strange way I'm better than ever, each of them by my side. I can smell pine trees. Even with the strip of pink pollution on the horizon, the stars stab through. I gulp the air, throw my head back. I have never felt so light.

— — —

We stay another day, mostly because we're feeling lazy. I fish out another seventy dollars from the wad I got from Uncle and give it to the receptionist, who doesn't even put it in a cash register but puts the folded bills into her pocket. I do the calculations: Carlos has about two hundred dollars on him. There's my mother's bank account—about three thousand—the cash from her bag and from Mr. Mehta—another twenty-one hundred. If we're careful, we can keep going. Stay on the road.

This time we go out for groceries—peanut butter and jam and bread, hard-boiled eggs, a bag of chips, and baby carrots. Carlos had the good sense to bring a soccer ball, and we also stop off at a dollar store and buy a Frisbee and a cheap plastic bat and balls. We find a small triangular park and play with Kamal, so he's laughing and throwing himself on the ground each time he catches the Frisbee. We do this until the tree shadows lengthen on the grass and the rest of the families are picking up and leaving. This time we go to a Red Lobster, where they have an all-you-can-eat buffet, and we eat so much our stomachs ache and back at the motel, all we can do is moan happily on the beds. Already this feels like a real vacation, lazing through my limbs like thick honey.

Turning on my phone, I see a stream of messages and texts from Lidia. *Status? You promised me. One day.* Then I check my emails and see a message from Amirah, the bookstore manager. *Just confirming you'll be available for training later this summer?*

I show Carlos the email. "What am I supposed to tell her? I didn't even tell my mom about this job."

"You didn't want to, did you?"

I look at him in surprise. My cheeks go warm again. It's as if Carlos were seeing right through me. How could he know me when he doesn't know me? And yet there's something old and familiar between us. I write her back, *Will get back to you soon.* I switch the phone off. Then I jump up, hoping he doesn't notice that I'm blushing, and say sternly to Kamal, "Time for a bath."

He jams his arms against his chest. "It's ugly in there."

"So are you," I tease.

I go and run the water and even though he makes a wrinkly nose, he does take a bath. To my relief, Kamal hasn't had any accidents since we got on the road. I'd been a little weirded out, sleeping next to him.

While Kamal is in the bathroom, Carlos and I sit on the floor, backs against the bed, and go back to flicking through the TV stations. The news is the same awful stuff: chaos at the border. Kids sobbing for their parents. Carlos looks drawn and tired, older.

"What about your aunt?" I ask. "Have you heard from her?"

"She's back in Mexico. They put her on a plane."

"What are you going to do?"

"Not sure. Someone told me Canada is better. I think I have a cousin there."

We go back to watching. His body is solid next to mine. I almost reach for his hand. Then he snaps the news off.

— — —

Carlos has woken before us, showing up with a cardboard tray of juice and doughnuts. "Let's go to a museum," he says. "There are really good ones in Boston."

Kamal groans into his pillow.

"This is an educational vacation, silly," I say, and teasingly flick a finger on his nose.

My phone has a cache of new messages—everything I've been avoiding. Lidia is frantic. "You're with your uncle? You need to get in touch ASAP. What about the form?" Then there's one from Ammi, who sounds strangely heartened. "That's my girl," she says, laughing. "Smarter than those shelter people. I told Lidia not to worry. You would figure out what to do." The last is from Fatima. "Please, Rania, tell me what's going on. I'm scared."

This cuts me, sharp. I text her: *Promise. Will call soon. Will explain.*

She texts back a sad-face emoji.

I've never gone so long without speaking to my best friend. But it's different now. I think of our T-shirts, the road making everything smaller and smaller until it's only a dot. That's what I want: to disappear, to turn it into freedom. I shut the phone off. We'll use Carlos's phone to navigate. And we'll just keep going, not looking back.

— — —

The Museum of Fine Arts in Boston is beautiful, with a huge atrium and different galleries branching off. Kamal is glum at first—he'd hoped we'd do Legoland—but I let him use my phone for a game and even interest him in a painting or two.

Carlos is the one to lead. He's clear on exactly what he wants to see. We wind up in front of a painting called *Dos Mujeres (Salvadora y Herminia)*. It's of two women, one in the front and the other just behind her, like two playing cards. Their hair is jet-black, pulled back sleekly with a part in the middle, their eyebrows thick brushes. The woman in the front has on a blue dress with a double-frill white yoke, gold hoops in her ears. Behind them is an olive-toned forest of leaves and fruit and butterflies. But the women are the most colorful things in the painting, their faces strong, their eyes gazing firmly. It makes me think of Ammi, her strength, and for an instant, I feel a wisp of sadness.

Then I realize this might be a mother and daughter. The woman in back wearing the yellow dress has an older face. It's really the daughter who's more vivid, her lips pink, her eyes hard black.

I am behind you always, Ammi used to say, especially when she was working extra Uber shifts and left us our dinner under damp towels. *Even when I can't be.*

Maybe I don't want Ammi behind me.

— — —

After, as we're sitting outside on a bench and eating our sandwiches, Carlos explains that the painting is by Frida Kahlo, a Mexican painter whose husband was the famous muralist Diego Rivera. But it's Kahlo's work he's always liked, how she often painted herself and turned her insides out for the world to see. He shows me a drawing he had been working on in his sketch pad using pastels: It's a portrait of himself. He's staring over his shoulder, and his two scars are carried up and over his head into a curved horn of birds and twisting branches and streaked sky. "Wow," I say. He explains that in art class last year they had to do a series that drew inspiration from famous artists.

"Did you know she had, like, twenty-six operations and lived with a metal bar in her body?" He points, as if tracing the outline of the women. "She painted out all that pain and stuff that happened to her. She turned her scars into beauty."

I want to fling my arms around Carlos's neck. A ticklish warmth slides through me. He makes me look at things from the inside out, through his quiet gaze. I'm not sure what he is to me, to us, but I've never felt something like this. I want to protect him and be protected by him.

— — —

"One more round, hermanito. To look at a few things."

Kamal stamps his foot, exasperated, points to the Frisbee. Carlos kneels down, puts his hand on Kamal's shoulder, and says softly, "You don't want to be a disappointment to me, do you?" I'm struck by how formal Carlos can be sometimes. Whenever I thank him for something small, like picking up a ball from the ground, he always answers, "My pleasure." He sounds like a waiter or a butler in a movie. I even ribbed him about it once. "Is that cultural or something?" He just replied, "That's the way I was taught."

The way. What is Carlos's way? He's a mix between an old-school gentleman and a street-smart kid, maneuvering through so many harrowing situations. The few times I've dared touch him, his muscles were taut, corded with tension. He stands some distance away, keeping a space between himself and others.

Kamal bites his lower lip, and Carlos continues. "Then you're going to hold my hand and we are going to walk quietly to the place that I want to go to. And you're going to stay and look with me. And when we're done—only then—we can go and get an ice cream and find a park and play, okay?"

"Okay!" Kamal grins.

We go to another gallery that has another artist he likes, Edward Hopper. "You're seeing my whole art class." Carlos laughs.

They are mostly drawings, a few paintings. Some feel lonely—a drawing of a house all by itself on a street. When I say this to Carlos, he agrees. "That's what I like about his work. He shows me how lonely it can be here."

A painting catches my eye, since it's so familiar: a wall of windows with faded-green blinds, looking over the tops of low, redbrick buildings. There's a woman with her back to us, sitting in a rocking chair, and a vase of flowers. *Room in Brooklyn,* it's called. "Hey, Kamal, look," I say. "Home."

But he's pulled close to some paintings of boats and white clapboard houses against a horizon, and a lighthouse on a bluff. "I want to go there," he says. "I want to see that."

Carlos and I look at each other. "Why not?" we both say.

— — —

Carlos finds another lighthouse on the internet, from a painting he remembers. We stop at a big supermarket and buy ourselves a Styrofoam cooler and a bag of ice, and load up on food for the road—sliced meats and cheese, grapes and bananas. Carlos eats bananas like there's no tomorrow. "I'm a growing boy," he says, patting his stomach. I also get myself a phone card.

I realize I've got to do something fast about Lidia. So I sign the folded form with my uncle's name, and fake the two witnesses—one of them Shaima, another a made-up person. I take a picture and text it to her along with: *Pls send Ammi's address PA.* This buys me time, but not much. They'll never know: Uncle is leaving soon enough. And I can feel Ammi egging me on, proud at how I'm outsmarting others. Run, she would say. Don't let anyone hold you back.

Soon I get a message from Lidia. *About time! OK for now. Uncle may need court appearance.* A few minutes later she sends an address in Pennsylvania. Relief washes through me. We can keep going. For now.

While Carlos and Kamal go to the bathroom, I call Fatima with my phone card. She starts to cry and yell at me that her parents are furious, that her father doesn't want her to have anything to do with me. "Where are you?"

I just listen. "I can't tell you."

"You don't trust me."

I consider this a moment. "It's not that. What if Lidia or the shelter people call you and ask a lot of questions? All I can tell you is we're traveling. On the road."

"Like in the novel? With a boy? That should be me and you!"

"Fatima, this is different. It isn't some joyride, okay? I don't have a choice."

"I just want to be with you."

I sigh. "I miss you too, Fa-Fa. But this is serious. We're running for real."

She is quiet. Then she whispers, "Ra-Ra, I'm scared. You don't even know this boy."

"He's okay."

"How do you know?"

I pause. How do I know? I think of the cinnamon bun with melting icing, the way he so naturally plays with the little kids. Or what he said when he showed me the painting. He saw right into me almost from the start. That ticklish feeling starts in my chest, spools outward, to all of me. He knows what it's like to be unprotected. To always be on the run. There's an understanding quiet between us.

"Carlos is chill," I say softly. "He really is."

"He better be. Or I'll come and kick his ass." I hear her sniffling on the other end. "Get me something cool? Wherever you are?"

"I promise, Fa-Fa," I say.

— — —

Then we're heading out of Boston, toward Cape Cod.

"This way you can see the very tippy tip of America," Carlos explains to Kamal.

"What else can we do?"

"We can swim."

"In the ocean?"

"Yes."

His nose wrinkles. "Are there sharks?"

"Maybe. But that's why you have to be a fast swimmer."

"I need a floatie," he says. "I can't swim without a floatie!" Kamal is a cautious swimmer. We once took a few days off and Ammi drove us to a lake upstate; Kamal spent a lot of time on the beach, knees pressed together, not trusting the orange floaties on his arms.

I reach over and rub Kamal's ankle. "Don't worry. We'll swim where there are no sharks. And we'll get you a floatie."

I'm already liking this trip: after about an hour we're starting to pass buildings with cutouts of cheerful lobstermen in boats on the roofs, floats and blow-up rowboats swinging from the front porches. It feels like we're heading into a real vacation. Once we're crossing the Sagamore Bridge and see the glittering water, and then on Route 6, with its low shrubs and flat land, I open the windows to see if I can smell the sea, the way I did in Karachi, with Ammi and Abu.

Leaning over, Carlos tucks my hair back, which is flying into my eyes. "It never stays in place," he murmurs.

My face tingles, feeling his fingers against my skin. Then I call out, "Route Six!"

"So?"

"That's it! The whole way *On the Road* begins! He's in search of Route Six, which goes clear across the continent. Road America!"

Carlos laughs. "Whatever."

"Say it, both of you!"

Kamal makes a face and Carlos grumbles, but they chorus: "Road America!"

"Road America!" we all chant, happy.

— — —

Carlos keeps checking on Airbnb listings but there's nothing we could afford, and anyway, we can't trick the system into believing we're the right age. So we start pulling into motels. "No vacancy," a girl tells me and points to the sign out front. At a place with little cabins, the woman takes one look at my driver's license and snaps it on the counter. "Sorry. Your parents need to be with you."

We get in the car and keep going, down the long thin road, passing gray-shingle buildings selling lobster rolls and fried clams, miniature-golf places. The lighthouse we are aiming for is still miles ahead, in a town called Truro, but we figure any place to stay along the way will work.

As we're slowing near what looks like a motel, without a sign, we see two young women close to our age walking on the side of the road, holding plastic bags.

"Hey," Carlos calls. "Any room there?"

They look at each other. One has blond-streaked hair pulled into a ponytail; the other wears fringed denim shorts. "That's for the people who work here. At the restaurant." She has a thick accent—something European. She points to what looks like an old pancake house.

"Everyone?"

"If not there, they work the other restaurants."

The blonde clomps toward us. She looks very cool: She's wearing cowboy boots and shorts that sag at her hips. A tattoo flowers up her arm and around her shoulder. She too has an accent. "A girl who was supposed to come never made it." She turns to her friend. "I heard Doris say she has to figure out what to do with the room."

We find Doris pushing a rubber tub on wheels, spray cleaners hooked to the lip. Her face has a kind look, folding into a smile. "This place is meant for the kids who work around here," she explains. "I can work," Carlos says. "Delivery, busboy. Anything."

She gives him a dubious look but I can see she likes his take-charge energy.

"I guess so. But this isn't a Marriott or anything. Rooms are cleaned just once a week. You get new towels and that's it. Laundry is around the back—get yourself lots of quarters. And pay me cash or Venmo. That's better."

"Thank you!" I exclaim.

"Don't thank me," she says. "Thank the girl who never showed."

She pushes off, the spray canisters jiggling on the side of her tub.

— — —

Everyone who lives here is in their twenties. They come from places like Bulgaria and the Czech Republic and Macedonia and Poland to work the summer season. It's a special program where they get a temporary visa. A whole group of them work at the next-door restaurant, which is no longer a pancake house but serves a huge buffet. I hear them early in the morning—marching across the gravel driveway, then later their accented voices—"More scrambled eggs! Out of muffins! Someone take out the garbage!" By midday they return, limp and greasy, their showers throbbing through the thin walls. After, they sit out around the small swimming pool on the folding chairs and gossip, the girls with the insides of their pale arms turned up, faces tilted to the sun. All of them adore Kamal.

"He's so cute!" the girl in the fringed denim shorts squeals.

"I want those curls," her blond friend adds.

They bring us the food that isn't taken, so we eat well—cold eggs and quiche and sausages and muffins. They give us a map too, showing what beaches we can use, and if we can fork over the money, Doris will give us a piece of paper to get our beach and pond stickers too.

On our third day on the Cape, we drive to the lighthouse. Carlos brings his sketch pad and Kamal bounds ahead. We pay for our tickets and climb up the twisting steps until we're at the very top, gazing out over scrub brush and a rolling golf course and beyond, the Atlantic Ocean, flat and shiny blue, surrounding us. Then I remember staring at the Google map, how Cape Cod curls around like a great arm, jutting out into the water but somehow embracing too.

Kamal leans into me. I put my arm around him, pull him close. "I want to stay," he whispers.

Stay. It sinks into me, this new pebble-word.

"It's perfect," Carlos says. "We're, like, at the end of the earth. No one's going to find us here. We can hide out."

He shuts his eyes, and I notice the fringe of his lashes, golden brown.

Another word: *hide.*

— — —

Carlos talks to Dimitri, our neighbor in the next room, who's a cook at the restaurant and plays guitar in the evenings on the concrete patio. He sets Carlos up with busing and working the kitchen. "There's also delivery," he says. "You got a car." Carlos wakes early, like the others, and is part of the crunching footsteps in the morning, returning with more leftovers than we can stuff into ourselves. Since we have a car, unlike everyone else, our neighbors ask us to take them to the supermarket or the pharmacy, and they pay us five bucks for the gas or buy some extra PowerBars and snacks for us. And Carlos does a few deliveries, so he brings in a hundred bucks a day, which we store in an old mayonnaise jar. Not bad. There's still our tucked-away cash and Ammi's small savings account.

I drive into town and buy another phone card. Then I get nervous: If I speak to Ammi, might she ask to speak to Salim Uncle? I decide to get a postcard, something super-generic, so they won't guess where we are. I find one with sailboats in a harbor and write: *Dear Ammi, we are having a great time. Thank you for telling us to go to Uncle and Auntie. They are very nice. They say maybe we can take some trips together here in New England. I hope you are well. I know you will get out soon. Lidia is working on it. Kamal sends his love. Rania.* But then I realize I can't send it—what if she notices the Wellfleet stamp? Will she wonder? I shove everything into the bottom of my bag.

The next day, Doris knocks on my door. "Honey, I need to see your license if you're going to keep on here."

I go to the bureau and slowly hand the license to her, sucking in my breath while she peers at it. Her usually friendly expression creases for a moment. I get the prickly feeling all over my skin, and my stomach turns to jelly.

"Please," I beg.

Her eyes are sharp—sharper than I've ever seen. "You're not in trouble, are you?"

"No," I say. "We're just waiting. For my mom. Then we'll

all be together." It's a lame way of putting it, but I had to think quickly.

"That Carlos boy, he's a good kid. I hear he's a hard worker."

"I can work too," I put in.

Here she gets alert. "You don't mind cleaning toilets?"

I do, but I say, "My mom says I made ours shine like a jewel."

"Thatta girl. You come with me on Thursday and I'll show you what to do."

Once I started cleaning, I knew we could stay.

Chapter Thirteen

It's the second week of July and we're hiding out in this place that feels like it's the edge of America. Everything flat as can be, land and water reaching in all directions. We float along, disappearing inside the rhythms of mostly white families taking their vacations. The crowds are getting thicker around the fried fish places and lobster restaurants. The past two Saturdays there's been a slow caravan of cars crawling down Route 6, luggage tied to the roofs, bicycles spinning on the backs.

We pretend. We pretend we're not running because now we're staying. We pretend there's no news or headlines or sounds of children crying at shelters. We pretend there isn't a ripped seam in our families, from long ago, in another country.

Sometimes I worry if people wonder who we are—three brown-skinned kids, no adults around. But there are others like us: boys who bike over for their kitchen jobs in a cook's white pants or the restaurant's T-shirts; women who pop out of vans, hauling tubs of cleaning equipment, heading into rental homes. Once one of them called out to Carlos, "¡Hola!" and he gave a friendly wave back. We hide among them too.

I spoke to Ammi once and told her Uncle is busy working all

the time. I keep fending off Lidia, who is not happy. Ammi has put her off us, told her I'm responsible, with relatives. Sometimes I see Ammi's number lighting up my phone and I let it go to voice mail. *Sorry, Ammi,* I text. *Busy with Auntie. Helping out.* She texts back, *Good girl.* And finally I emailed Amirah, praying that I hadn't lost the job. *Sorry for the delay. Is it possible to do training in August? Can't wait to start!*

I can make our money stretch. On Wednesdays and Fridays, I let Kamal play video games on my computer while I don rubber gloves, push a laundry tub into each motel room, scrub the toilets and sinks and tubs, and leave stacks of fresh towels, which brings in another two hundred. And we get lots of free leftovers from the restaurant, which we store in the portable fridge. We buy beach and pond stickers, bathing suits, beach towels, plastic buckets, and arm floaties for Kamal, head out onto Route 6, and turn down the road, to a pond.

"Look, look!" Kamal shouts.

"I'm looking," I say.

It's perfect for him. There's a small sandy beach sloping toward the water's edge. A floating dock, where clusters of children are jumping into the pond. Kamal lets me rub him with lotion. He slides on his floaties and then stands with his ankles in the shallows. There are so many kids—all ages—splashing and tossing rubber balls and kicking in little round tubes. I sit on our towel and just watch Kamal, smiling at his bony back, the way he tentatively skims his fingers on the surface. I don't push him. Slowly he goes deeper, up to his calves, then his knees. I can tell it's super shallow because it takes a while to get up to his shoulders. And then suddenly, he's in, thrashing around in his awkward dog paddle, his orange floaties flashing in the sun. I lie down on my towel, content.

— — —

A shadow falls across my eyes.

"Hey."

A guy is standing over me. My blood jumps. Then I realize it's Carlos. He drops down beside me. I've never seen him in a bathing suit—his is navy blue with white stripes and a too-big drawstring that cinches around his narrow waist. He's just come off a shift and walked here. I can see sweat beading around his neck. His hair curls sweetly around his ears. They are delicate, elfin.

"That's a long walk," I say.

"I've walked longer."

He's in one of his moods. Carlos gets those sometimes. I figure it's because he's thinking about his aunt. Or what he's doing next. He ducks into silence or brings out his drawing pad and soon gets lost in his work. He told me he loves this landscape, the scrub pine with their gnarly branches mirrored, upside down, in the shimmering ponds. There's no prying a word out of him. I've brought my notebook too, scribbling down thoughts, sputters of writing.

"This is great, isn't it?" I ask.

"Yeah."

"Wouldn't it be cool if we could do this always?"

"What do you mean?"

"Maybe you can earn some money off your drawing. We

could make books together. I'll write the captions. We'll sell them. And—"

"Rania," he warns. "Let's just be here for now. Okay?"

"Okay."

We go back to our work, but I'm feeling jumpy, unable to concentrate. I can't stand his silence anymore, so I ask, "What arc you going to do?"

"Do about what?"

"Your situation."

He goes back to his drawing, hand cupped around a charcoal nub. My heart is galloping in my chest, as I think, I have to help him. I'll call Lidia. She'll figure something out. But when I tell him my idea, he puts a hand on my arm. "Rania, stop. It's better this way. No plans. We'll figure it out."

He leans back on his elbows and closes his eyes. I can see he's exhausted. He works a lot more hours than I do. "Papers, no papers," he mumbles. "What's the difference in the end?"

"But—"

"Learn to wait, Rania."

"I'm not good at waiting."

"No kidding."

"I just don't understand how this could happen to us," I say. "We followed the rules. We're not even undocumented."

He slams his drawing pad down. "¡No chingues! The only difference between you and me is a good lawyer, Rania."

Rolling over, he shows me his back. Tears sting my eyes. I want to stroke the bony line of his spine, make it better between us, but my hand won't budge.

"Are we having our first fight?" I whisper.

His voice is muffled. "No, Rania. I'm just tired, okay?"

"Okay. Sorry."

I get up, walk into the pond, wading toward Kamal, and play with him awhile, letting him jump up into my arms. "Do you want to go to the dock?" I ask.

He bites his lip. "It's too far."

"I can carry you."

He considers this. Kamal always weighs what he wants to do—he never likes to be pushed. "Next time, okay, Aapi?"

Smiling, I half twirl him back in, so he splashes, giggling. Then he drifts over to a group of kids tossing a plastic ball, so I decide to swim out, past the dock.

I was always a swimmer—it came naturally to me—the breathing, hands slicing the surface. One summer Ammi signed me up at the Y, and that was that. But I've never swum a place like this—open, without buoys marking the lanes. Ahead are blotches of darker water, the reflection of bushes along the shore, stabbing downward. I aim toward them. The farther I go, the more I can feel my own strength, pulling from my stomach. I swim until the sandy beach shrinks to a flat line and the kids are just dots on the dock. The water feels like silk, folding around me. But then I picture Kamal's worried little face, and turn back. I swim harder, with purpose. I'm going to help Carlos. Somehow.

When I reach our towel, I lean down, kiss Carlos awake on the cheek. A surge of warmth springs loose inside me. Was that the right thing to do?

His eyes flutter open, surprised. He is smiling. He's not mad at me! Just then, Kamal races up and plows into his stomach. "Oof!" Carlos grunts, then laughs and tackles my brother.

We crank open the car windows, let the breeze skim our still-wet skin, our hair, our fingers. Carlos is relaxed. We decide to splurge and treat ourselves to fried food in the pretty town, which curves down a hill with galleries and little shops that sell mugs and T-shirts and beaded bracelets that cost too much. The restaurant sits right on the bay, the water jeweled and shiny from the lowering sun. All around us are families, mostly white families, though to my relief, I see a few South Asians. I see grandparents with wispy gray hair and striped nautical shirts, helping feed the kids. My eyes film with tears. We're a family too, I tell myself.

"So," I say to Carlos, as we push aside our empty food containers. "Just hear me out. What if Ammi gets out? You can come live with us. You can be a delivery guy for Uber Eats. Like the ones who scooter around in yellow vests with the insulated bags on the back."

He tilts his head, amused. "You don't give up, do you?"

"They will totally love you, all the people who work at the restaurants—"

Kamal brightens. "Is Carlos staying with us in Brooklyn?"

Carlos laughs and stands. "Hermanito, it's time for ice cream. Not talk."

As I watch them walk away to the ice cream window, my heart soars. They do belong together: lanky Carlos, one hand set lightly on Kamal's head while Kamal hops on one foot.

I'm lit up with plans: He'll meet Fatima and give her ideas for her fashion designs, and they'll argue over who is my best friend. We'll swim in the pool in Sunset Park, teach Kamal how to finally ride a bike. My mind is spinning. It will all work out.

I pull out the prepaid phone card and call Fatima and tell her my ideas about Carlos coming to live with us in Brooklyn.

"Whoa, whoa, Rania. Slow down. So now you're his savior?"

"No! I just think it would be so cool. He can go to art school. You to FIT—"

"I'm going to Brooklyn College," she points out.

"Okay, but we can be together."

She laughs. "Ra-Ra, I love you. But you get carried away. You think just because you dream something up, it can happen."

"I don't see why not."

"Hey, tell me about your uncle! What was *that* like?"

I flinch. "Complicated."

I'm not ready to tell her about my father. The past few nights, old memories of Pakistan have been bumping into my mind. I remember how my brand-new leather book bag squeaked when I ran down the street to school. I had a best friend then too— Asma—and she liked coming to my home because Ammi let us play nomads in a desert, making a tent, draping a quilt over the chairs in the middle of the living room, using brass goblets and plates for our meals. I miss that Ammi—the one who taught me how to dream and imagine with so little.

"Fatima, about my idea. What do you think?"

She sighs. "There are . . . limits. On what we can do."

"What does that mean?"

She's quiet—so unlike Fatima.

"Fa-Fa," I say. "Is something going on?"

I can hear her sucking in wet breaths. "My father says I have to go out with the boys they choose. Especially if I want to go to college. They want things settled."

"Bullshit! You have to stand up to him. Remember, freedom—"

"What do you know!"

"Whoa, Fa-Fa—"

"I can't be like you! Doing whatever you like! Coming up with all kinds of fantastic stuff!"

There's a gulf opening up between us. Maybe it was there all along. I don't get why she doesn't stand up to her father. Fatima doesn't understand how my parents fought those old conservative ideas. Or the spike of fear I feel every time I see a local police car. That one day I'll turn on my phone and learn Ammi is gone. Deported. This is the first time I've kept something from Fatima.

I spot Carlos bringing Kamal back. His dyed streak is lighter from the sun and falls over his face as he leans toward Kamal, whispering some kind of joke. Every part of me wants to be next to him.

"I gotta go."

"Yeah, me too."

We hang up.

— — —

After, we drive to the ocean-side beach. I'm still upset with Fatima, and upset with myself. Why do I keep banging into conversations, hurting people? Dark falls swiftly as we clamber down the steep dunes. We walk and walk, passing clusters of bonfires, flames blowing thinly in the dark. Wind rubs our faces. The ocean looks like a midnight-blue sheet being shaken out, again and again, unfurling a few feet away.

Carlos and I sit down on the sand while Kamal keeps tossing flat stones in the water. He pushes my hair out of my eyes again, as it whips around. "Don't bother," I say, and laugh.

"I like doing it."

We fall quiet.

"Tell me about your aunt," I finally say.

I can barely make out Carlos, but I see him lean forward, arms cupped around his knees. "She was very good. She worked at a factory. For sixteen years. She led a quiet life. Went to church every Sunday. She was good to me. Even when I got in trouble at school, she didn't say she would send me back."

His chest sucks inward as he takes a breath. "And then one day they just showed up. Said her deportation order was in effect. And that was that. I was in gym at the time." He pauses. "Can you imagine? I was running around the track hoping this girl Lucinda didn't see how slow I was."

Carlos doesn't act like a regular teenager, with normal stupid obsessions. I'm stung with jealousy for a girl named Lucinda watching Carlos run laps. Is that who he's thinking about? Why he holds himself back from me? I bite down on the thought. We're like a mom and dad, taking care of Kamal. A brother and sister. Not a boyfriend and girlfriend. Then why do I stare at his mouth when he talks, wishing I could kiss him? Why do I want to smooth those thin scars with my fingers?

"How is she now?"

"She's back in our town. I spoke to her a few times. She told me those guys—the ones who made me run—they keep asking about me."

"What does she tell them?"

"That I'm never coming back." His voice goes tight. "And I'm not."

I keep watching the jerking silhouette of Kamal tossing his stones.

"Don't you ever get angry?" I ask. "At all that's happened to you?"

"Not anymore. That gets you nowhere." He turns to me. "The solution will come."

"Paciencia."

"That's why I like to draw. It makes me slow down. Take things in. Especially when there's so much shit I can't control."

I think about what Fatima said. How I've always thought I could push through anything. Just like Ammi. I've watched her barge into offices, demanding all the right documents so she could get a license. She doesn't take no for an answer. Neither do I. But sometimes having a will is not enough. Here we are: She's stuck in some awful detention center. Me and Carlos and Kamal in a motel room, suspended. Waiting.

"Okay, your turn," Carlos says. "What about your father?"

"What about him?" I'm aware of Carlos's leg, right next to mine, electric with warmth.

"Are you going to do anything?"

"He's no one," I say. My throat feels hoarse.

But I mean it. Ever since Uncle told me about my real father, I've pushed him far down in my mind. I think about the way I snuck glances at Uncle, combing for traits that connected him to me. His nose, his mouth, his neck. Particles, cells, genes. What does that even mean? Is that family? I haven't told Carlos about the new memories that have begun edging into my thoughts.

Carlos rears up from his haunches and hurls a pebble to the water's edge. "Nobody!" he shouts. "He's nobody!"

Kamal, hearing us, twists around and repeats, "Nobody!"

"Stop!" I laugh and also heave myself up from the sand. I fling my arms around him and give him a kiss. His cheek is rough, cool. In the dark I can't see his reaction, because he's turning, calling for Kamal, his back to me.

Back in the motel, there's an awkward strain between us. I feel idiotic, hot with shame for what I've done. Not just once, but twice. I better stop.

"Good night, Rania," he says, like every night, and snaps out his light.

Chapter Fourteen

When I wake, Carlos is gone. But then he doesn't come back after the morning shift, not even to bring us leftovers. I don't know what to think. Who are we to each other? Is he my almost-boyfriend or did I drive him away? I feel like an idiot. Just what Fatima says: always thinking I can just will something to happen. It's like I've taken my lace-up boots and tromped on something delicate and sweet.

I look around the room. He's taken his backpack with his sketch pad and charcoal and pencils. But his pictures are everywhere: taped to the walls, propped on the bureau, fluttering near a vent. They're of the oblong stretches of dune grass, the kids jumping off the dock at the pond, of us and even Dimitri, the cook in the restaurant. Carlos's stroke is sure, and he hones in on a telling detail, like the worry-crease in Kamal's forehead, or how Dimitri keeps one hand tucked behind his back as he flips a pancake.

I crack open the window blinds, searching for him. It nags at me: Carlos does need help. We can't just wait.

I try to busy myself with my emails. Nothing from Fatima,

which makes the ache bore deeper. A lot about fall semester at Hunter—what courses I want to sign up for, clubs I can join.

Kamal is getting bored, staying in the motel room. Snapping the laptop shut, I head over to the kitchen, where they give me some day-old muffins. I'm crossing the driveway when I spot Doris talking to a strange man. I freeze. He's got on a suit, which is odd here on the Cape, and carries a folder. He scribbles something down, then gets into a car and backs out of the lot.

I walk over to Doris. "Who's that?"

"Some guy from immigration. Bill."

Maybe Lidia did get the word out. Or the shelter did.

"Came over from Boston to check on the kids," Doris continues. "Make sure all their papers are in order. They do that sometimes." She swipes at her hair. "He asked about you guys."

Ice slides into my stomach.

"I told him you're here for a little while, your ma is coming soon." She peers at me. "When is that again?"

"Soon," I reply and duck into the room, trying to act calm as I hand Kamal his muffin. He makes a face. "It's too dry!"

"Too bad."

"I don't like raisins."

"Deal with it, Kamal!"

I rush into the bathroom, slam the door. My whole body feels like it's breaking. Calm down, I tell myself. Calm. Then I call Lidia.

"Where are you?" she asks.

"With my uncle," I lie.

"Listen, it's pretty unorthodox how the form was handled.

I need to speak to him. It will be better if we formalize this in court—"

"He's really busy with work," I say. "He . . . he went on a business trip."

"When does he get back?"

"I don't know." I rub my tongue over my teeth. It's amazing how easy lying has become. One into another. Just like the grown-ups.

"Your mother was asking."

"It's okay. We're with family."

I'm staring at myself in the mirror, waiting for the panic to pass. I can see faint strap marks from my bathing suit. I ask, "Can I ask you a favor?"

"I suppose." Her voice is cautious.

"If you had a client, a kid, who was living with his aunt and she got deported and he's all alone—"

"Rania—" Lidia warns.

"I'm just asking!"

"Are you with that boy? The one from the shelter?"

I pause, my pulse skittering. "We're in touch," I say.

"He's in big trouble, you know."

"I didn't know," I say faintly.

And then I can't help myself: I tell her how great Carlos is, how talented, how unfair it is that he doesn't have a lawyer. That he crawled across the desert in the middle of the night and he can't go back, not ever. When I'm done, there's quiet on the other end.

"You sound like you're in love with him."

My skin prickles, all over. "I am not."

She laughs. "Okay, you're in like."

"He's a friend. And he's all alone." I add, "I have Kamal. And Ammi." Then, "And now my uncle."

She sighs. "So what are you asking?"

"Will you be his lawyer?"

Her silence is longer than I like.

--- --- ---

"Why did you tell that lady we're with Uncle?" Kamal asks when I come out of the bathroom.

I make a face at him. "You shouldn't be listening in on other people's conversations."

"Are we going back to see them?" he asks.

"Do you want to?"

"I want to play with Roshaan and Maira."

I look at him. He's sitting on the bed, kicking his feet against the spread. I feel badly—all these changes, the stories I make up on the fly. "Get dressed," I say. "I changed my mind. You can have fried clams again."

"And ice cream?"

"You're pushing it."

Carlos still hasn't returned, so I load up my backpack with towels, lotion, water, books. Act like it's a normal day.

I drive to town, where I find some generic New England postcards, already stamped. Dimitri, the cook, goes into Boston every week for supplies, so I'll ask him to mail them from there. We eat, Kamal happily dipping his clams in sauce. I squeeze some lemon on them, tell him that's the way to get some Vitamin C. Then I take out a postcard and write: *Dear Ammi, we miss you very much. We're good. Kamal is eating and growing and having a great time. I can't wait to see you soon. Love, Rania.*

"Who are you writing to?" Kamal asks.

"A friend."

"Why don't you text?"

"She collects postcards."

"Fatima?"

This stabs me. I check my phone. No message. I've ruined everything: with her. And with Carlos, all because of a stupid kiss. Not even a *real* kiss.

"Hey."

There's Carlos, his backpack angled over his shoulder. Relief sweeps through me but I tamp down the urge to hug him.

Kamal's face brightens. "Carlos!"

I scrunch to the side of my chair, as he joins us, pops a fried clam into his mouth. "Man, these are good."

"Where were you?" I keep the scowl out of my voice.

"Ernie asked me to join him on some supply pickups." He bends toward Kamal and taps his bicep. "Me, strong," he teases. "Lift fifty-pound sack."

Kamal giggles, but I say, "Why didn't you tell me?"

He gives me a blank look. "I was working, Rania. It's money."

I squash down my hurt.

"You want to go on a trip?" he asks.

"We're on a trip," I grumble.

"Trip!" Kamal chimes.

I don't really have a choice since Carlos has Kamal excited. We pay up and I slide the postcard into my bag. Next time I'll write one without lies.

— — —

What Carlos means is a drive to Provincetown, which is at the very tip of the Cape. It's a kitschy town with narrow, crowded streets, T-shirt stores, and souvenir places. Rainbow flags flutter from most of the shops, and a man in a pink wig hands us a card to a drag show later that night. By the pier, families are lining up for the whale-watching boats. Still I can't get rid of the nervous pulse in my body.

Leaving Kamal with Carlos, I go into one of the touristy shops, looking at sailboat mugs and napkin holders, placemats. Then my eyes light on the perfect item: long strings of tiny white seashells. I buy a whole bunch of them: a peace offering for Fatima. She'll figure out what to do with them. Not that I know if I'll ever see her again. I lean against a storefront, trying to compose myself. What did we get ourselves into?

Kamal comes running over. "Did you see?"

"What?"

"Carlos!"

I rush down the street to see that Carlos is by a low wall; he has his sketch pad out and is drawing a little girl. "He's good," the father comments.

Of course. Carlos has charmed someone into letting him draw them. Though it isn't easy: The girl is squirmy and keeps chewing on her saltwater taffy. A picture emerges of a sulky little girl with a turned-up nose and a bow-tie-shaped mouth. Pleased, the dad hands Carlos a twenty and tells him to keep it up. As we're leaving, a woman steps out of a little shop and shouts, "Hey!"

Carlos looks scared, pulling his head into his sweatshirt hood.

"I saw you drawing there!" Then we realize the woman, who introduces herself as Marge, is offering to let him set up in the alleyway right next to her shop.

Carlos's shoulders drop with relief. He isn't being accused of something. This is just like what he used to do, in Guanajuato—portraits of tourists. She shows us a little cobbled lane and folding chairs that he can use. "It would be my pleasure," he says.

Marge beams. "So well-mannered."

And so it's settled: Carlos will be back on the weekend after his restaurant shift; they'll charge thirty for a portrait, and Carlos negotiates for a 70 percent cut. We celebrate with a dinner at an outdoor dockside restaurant, the three of us sharing a lobster roll, mayonnaise dripping down our fingers, and a captain's special of fried fish and clams. A ruddy sun is dipping down on the horizon, swelling the water in vibrant hues. "Can we go on the whale boats?" Kamal asks.

"Yes," Carlos says automatically.

"They're expensive," I warn.

He motions to his sketch pad. "I'm a working man! Making money from drawing, just like you said!" He lightly punches my arm.

I give him a feeble grin back. So I'm just a buddy.

As we're finishing, my phone dings; there's a message from Lidia: *OK. You win. I'll help Carlos. Send me info and I'll see what I can do. No promises. Have your uncle call me!*

I shift over to Carlos, who is standing by the big boats that go out on whale-watching trips, telling Kamal that they can go next week. Sometimes I think Carlos spoils Kamal because it's as if he's giving the kid a life that got interrupted for him.

I tell him, "She'll do it."

He looks puzzled. "Do what?"

"Lidia will represent you!"

He pulls away. "That's okay." He's hunched over, kicking at the posts. "I don't need you to help me. To feel sorry for me."

My temples throb. "Is that what you think this is?"

"Isn't it?" He turns to me, his face looking gaunt in the shadows. "Poor little Mexican boy. Like all those kids they show every night on the news? You want to rescue me?"

My eyes sting with tears. "You must be kidding."

"I'm not." His voice is cold. "Have you seen my drawings? The ones I did in the shelter? Did you notice I never show them crying or clutching their stuffed animals? It makes me sick. The way they show us, night after night. Always with the eyes of pity. I will never be that." He lifts his chin.

"God, you are so . . . arrogant! You want to turn down a perfectly good offer? Lidia is awesome."

"Really? If she's so great, how come your mother's in that place?"

"That is so unfair," I say softly. My ribs hurt, as if someone had punched them, hard.

He's quiet, staring out at the boats, hands jammed in his sweatshirt pockets. "Look, I'm used to being on my own. Doing it my way." He gives a sly smile. "Like that lady there. I got her to seventy percent. Not bad."

"But—"

"Stop."

I watch him head toward the lot where the car is parked. I hate him sometimes. But sometimes too I feel as if I were looking at a mirror of myself: proud, armored, too self-sufficient. Grown up fast. *We're the same!* I want to yell. But we don't say anything the whole way back to the motel, the gray road humming before us, Kamal draped across the back seat, asleep. And as I slide into bed that night I don't know what hurts the most: that Carlos won't take my help. Or that he won't kiss me back.

Chapter Fifteen

We may be in blazing summer heat, we may be earning more money, but Carlos and I are barely talking.

For the next week we keep to our routines: He does his restaurant work; I help out at the motel. We steer around each other in the small room. Sometimes in the morning when I'm gathering my clothes, I see Carlos sneak a glance at me. I slam the bathroom door. Or he reaches to brush aside my hair, then yanks his hand back. The worst part is the only person I want to confide in is Fatima, but she still hasn't answered my texts, which kills me. Her shells stay tucked in my bag. At least Bill, the immigration guy, hasn't returned.

I push myself to swim all the time. Paciencia. Waiting. I go farther out into the pond toward those patches of dark green, slashing the water with my arms, furious at him, at us, at all I can't change.

On Saturdays, after Carlos's shift, we pile into the car and drive to Provincetown where Carlos draws tourists in the little alley. Kamal and I climb Pilgrim Monument, ticking off the names of the early settlements—Springfield, Hartford, Providence—carved into its walls. Marge adores Carlos, tells him he's welcome to come other days too. I think about how welcoming everyone here has been—Doris and Jeff, the manager of the restaurant. Another America, not the one that sent Ammi down the stairwell of our building that night; not the one on the news.

We both spoil Kamal. We play miniature golf. We buy him cheap toys that break after a day. A Styrofoam kickboard that he uses—all the way to the floating dock. "Hermanito, come to me!" Carlos calls from the water. Kamal jumps right into his arms, thrashing his way to shore. This is the part that makes me happy; we're giving him a childhood. The one that was snatched from us.

At the library, Kamal and I sit at a table and I spread out several postcards. "What do you think Ammi wants to hear?" I ask.

"That I'm swimming!"

"Good."

"I'm not afraid of sharks."

"Why don't you draw that?" Then I add, "But only that." I have to be careful because I don't want him to write about Carlos or the Cape. He clutches a pen and soon he's absorbed in doing his letters and making a drawing, the tip of his tongue showing from concentrating so hard.

Missing you, Ammi.

Having a good summer, Ammi.

Can't wait until we see you, Ammi.

We'll be back soon, Ammi.

We live on lies the same way we live on the tufts of summer clouds and taffy and ice cream down at the dock. I never knew lying could taste so good. *Disappeared.* I think about that word, writing in my notebook.

But how much longer can we keep this up? Today I sign up for my classes, pay the utilities bill, watch Ammi's bank account slip down to twenty-five hundred. Our mayonnaise jar of crumpled bills covers our weekly expenses, and I've barely touched the cash. But we can't do this forever.

— — —

A rapping of knuckles on the doorjamb. Carlos stands there, grinning. "Hola, madam. Would you like to come to dinner with me?"

I look at him, surprised. "But what about the money?"

"Come on. We deserve a little break."

He's making a peace offering, I realize, so I shower, shake out my wrinkled graduation dress, and strap on my sandals. In the bathroom I put on kohl and some gloss and wrestle my hair into a bun, letting two curls dangle down my cheeks. When I step out, to my surprise, there's Carlos in a crisp white shirt and jeans, his hair slicked back.

"Wow," he says.

"Why do you look like that?" Kamal complains.

"Don't you think your sister's pretty?" Carlos asks.

My bare arms tingle.

"No," Kamal says. "She's just Rania."

Carlos laughs. "You need to remember to compliment your older sister, Kamal."

"You look good too. Guapo."

"Where'd you learn that?"

I shrug. "I'm a fast learner."

He blushes. "After you." He opens the door and sweeps an arm out.

We drop off Kamal with Dimitri, who will babysit, then drive into town and sit at a table at a restaurant overlooking the harbor. The waitress treats us like almost-grown-ups. We get appetizers—slippery oysters; I order broiled fish of the day while Carlos gets linguine with clams. The sun glances off the bobbing boat masts. We talk about silly things—gossip about the kitchen or Kamal's turning into a stronger swimmer. Nothing serious and Carlos is so polite I can't tell what this is—a date or an older-brother-sister treat? When our dessert of chocolate mousse arrives, I tell him about how upset I am with Fatima. "She ghosted me," I say.

"You're growing, that's all," Carlos says. "Like two stalks that lean to different suns."

"Always the artist," I tease.

"You're an artist too, Rania." He takes a last spoonful. "Don't get so caught up in the little things. Pay attention to the big stuff."

But I can't stop the urgent questions that pulse inside me. What about after the summer? My job? Ammi? Can Carlos be with us?

"Come," he says, setting down his napkin. "Let's pay and get the last of the sunset."

We drive over to a beach on the bay side. I undo my sandals and we traipse through the dunes, to watch the sky swell red, the marsh grasses darken. The air folds around us, velvety, soft.

"I've never felt such quiet," Carlos says.

I look at him, grateful, and let out a breath "Me neither."

It's true: everywhere I've lived has always been noisy and jammed. Here I can feel my breaths, my pulse slow. The sun arcs and spreads beneath the flat horizon. It feels like the last days of us. Whatever we are.

Carlos puts his arm around me, kisses the top of my head. "You are very special, Rania. Don't waste that."

Then he lets his arm go. The air blows between us. "We should get back to Kamal," he says.

As we trudge back to the parking lot, I feel Carlos watching me. His eyes follow my hands as I grab the clump of keys. "That lawyer lady have any news for you?" he asks.

"Nope."

"You going to find out about your father?"

"Why do you care?" I ask.

His eyes shimmer. "I do care, Rania."

"I don't want to talk about that," I mumble.

We get back in the car and drive in glum silence. I feel as if I'm breaking apart. Carlos looks miserable too.

— — —

The first Saturday in August, when Carlos is supposed to sketch, they predict lousy weather. Not raining, but the sky looks like an old washcloth leaking dirty gray water. We decide to do the whaleboat tour since Carlos figures there won't be many tourists in P-town. The boat is only half-full and we stand against the rail, mist drops spitting into our faces. The prow churns through choppy swells, its motion surging up from my feet through my legs.

The tour guide calls out to show us a few geysers of white

foam in the distance. Kamal jumps up and down, excited. "Look, Rania! Look, Carlos!"

Carlos hoists Kamal up to see better.

"Careful," I warn. The rocking is giving me a sour taste at the back of my throat.

Carlos smiles. He doesn't look as tired, the way he's been these last days. Summer has streaked his orange thatch of hair to blond. They are pointing and laughing.

"Another one!" Kamal squeals.

"It's a mother and baby," Carlos comments.

I nudge closer. Our shoulders bump, sending tiny bits of static through my arm. He hands me the binoculars the guide gave us. I squint and can just see the rounded back of the mother whale, then a little frothy spurt beside her. I hand them back.

"This is fun," he says. "Thank you."

"My pleasure," I tease.

He grins. "Impaciente. Right?"

I smile. "Sorry for the other day. When you asked about my dad." I look away. "It's kind of hard to talk about that stuff."

We stay at the rail, even as my stomach keeps cramping. I want to throw up but I make it back to shore. Back on land the rocking ripples up through my knees, as if we're still on the water. We eat but the food sits like a heavy balloon under my ribs.

As we're heading toward the lot, I say, "I don't feel so well."

"I can drive."

"You sure?"

"It's just a straight shot."

In the car, I close my eyes. My lids are burning. And I don't know why, but all the frustrations of the past few days boil up. Carlos is being nice, but why does he have to be so stubborn? "I don't get it," I say. "Everyone thinks you're so great. They'll help you."

"I told you already. I don't need help."

"Don't need or don't want?"

He doesn't answer.

"What are you going to do? You've got to get a lawyer. Lidia says—"

"Lidia this, Lidia that," he says in a singsong voice.

"You are such a jerk."

Carlos is gripping the wheel, and we go faster. Kamal starts to whimper. Next there's a blinding white light flaring into the rear window. A siren shrieks.

"Shit," Carlos says under his breath.

The siren wails again.

"What should I do?" His hands are trembling.

"Pull over," I whisper.

There's a crackling sound under the tires as we come to the shoulder. Carlos looks terrified, the color drained from his face.

A cop is leaning over, tapping the window with his knuckles. Carlos is frozen. The cop taps harder, angrier.

"Carlos," I whisper.

He can't move.

"Carlos," I beg. Kamal starts to cry.

Seeing Carlos unable to press the window switch, I make a flapping motion with my hands, to indicate *Yes, sir, we're on it*, and then I stretch across Carlos and press the window open.

But the cop is furious and snarls, "License! Registration!" His flashlight scans across the car interior. His mouth twitches when the beam sets on a frightened Kamal curled in the back.

I fumble in the glove compartment and find the little vinyl flap where Ammi keeps the registration and insurance card, and then I'm nudging Carlos in the arm, begging him to give his license.

"What's wrong with him?" the cop asks.

"He's scared," I say. "That's all."

"He was going seventy-five miles an hour."

"I'm sorry."

"Why are you sorry? He's the one that was driving."

At this, Carlos seems to stir. "Excuse me, officer." With a shaking hand he pulls out his wallet and hands it to him. Then he squeezes his eyes shut, his face pinched, as if he were bracing for someone to hit him. His right leg is bouncing, up, down, up down.

"You better step out."

"Sir?"

"Out."

Carlos unwinds himself from the seat belt and steps outside. My heart is thundering in my chest. Carlos: head bowed, shoulders hunched, hands at his sides. He looks like the men I watched being taken in ICE vans—their bodies surrendered. He looks nothing like the Carlos drawing tourists, teasing Kamal.

I leap out of the car and come around the front of the hood. I see another officer approaching from the patrol car.

"Whose car is this?" the cop asks.

"My mother's."

"Where is she?"

"She's . . . she's in New York. Brooklyn. She's working but she let us have the car—"

Frowning, the cop hands the license over to the other cop, who takes it inside their car. I can see he's punching something into the dashboard. The interior light makes his face look gaunt and gray, serious. The first cop makes Carlos walk a straight line. While he does, I keep babbling, telling him how it was my fault, that usually I drive but I wasn't feeling well because I got seasick on the whale boat.

"Where do you live?" the cop asks.

I stammer something about the motel. He looks skeptical, regards Carlos. Then the other cop comes back, hikes up his belt, and hands Carlos his license. "Nothing," he says, though he sounds as if he doesn't believe it.

"I'm not giving you a ticket," the first cop says.

"Thank you!" I exclaim.

He glares at me. "But this is a warning. No more joyriding on these roads. You got it?"

Carlos nods. He takes the license, shoves it into his pocket. We tramp back to the car. Poor Kamal is staring through the window.

"And get that kid to bed!" the other cop calls. "It's late!" They both laugh.

Their doors slam and then we get in the car, me in the driver's seat, Carlos slumped against his side, hood drawn up over his head. We turn back onto Route 6 in silence. My queasiness is gone. The black sky is stabbed with tiny stars.

Back at the motel we put Kamal to bed and then sit out on

the concrete patio. Fortunately, no one else is around. Carlos is holding his arms tight, rocking back and forth.

"What happened?" I whisper.

"I . . . I froze." I hear him suck in his breath. "When they came for my aunt, I wasn't home. But I knew they'd be back. Three times they came to the house. The cops knocked on the door. I hid out. But they got me the last time."

"That's how you came to the shelter?"

He nods. "When I was running back home, in Guanajuato, if we saw police, we just went the other way. We knew they were paid off." He rubs his face. "I am so . . . tired."

He sounds a million years old. Worn-out. Sick of running. This time I don't stop myself. I put my arms around him and nudge my face into his sweatshirt, which smells of soap and chalky pastels. His hood falls back to his neck. His skin is warm. And then we are hugging and kissing and crying too. We are mouths and hands and touch. But mostly we're holding each other, under the swarm of summer stars, on this thin spit of land at the very end of America, because we are all we have.

Chapter Sixteen

"You need to leave," Lidia tells me in the morning.

Carlos and I had fallen asleep in our clothes but I woke early in a panic. Last night came rushing back to me: the policemen, Carlos's shoulders bowed, his face pale and frightened. I can't hide anymore. We can't hide. I called Lidia and blurted out the truth: We weren't with my uncle. He signed the guardianship form but he left the country. We've been working on the Cape. She was furious, saying how dangerous and illegal this was, that I'd put her in a terrible spot as our mother's attorney. "I could wring your neck, Rania," she said. "Leave," she repeats. *"Now."*

"But where?" I look around our room—our beach bag, the squashed chip bags, Carlos's drawings and backpack splayed open with his sketch pad. He's left to do his breakfast shift. Kamal is still a sleeping lump in the bed. I think about all the people who have helped us here—Doris, Dimitri and the folks who work at the restaurant, Marge in P-town.

"Look. Do you understand how lucky you were? You say that immigration was poking around?"

"Yeah."

"I'm sure Carlos is in some kind of database. They just don't have the resources to connect to that. But you won't always be that lucky."

"You talk about him as if he's a criminal! He's just a kid. Like me!"

"Rania. Do you have any idea what's going on out there? They've got ICE officers showing up at the shelter." Her voice cracks. "I've never seen anything like it."

"You have to help us," I beg. "I'm scared."

"You should have been scared before." She says sternly, "You need to come back to New York."

"No."

"Rania—"

"We can't. They'll put us in the shelter."

I hear her sigh on the other end. Sunlight is starting to seep through the blinds. Kamal stirs. "Okay, look. There's this group I've heard of. In southern Vermont. They're not quite set up for situations like this, but I can talk to them."

"Please," I beg.

We hang up. I pace the motel room, then step outside, squinting into the sunshine. The mist has gone—already it's a hot day. Kamal will be up soon, begging to go to the beach or ponds. But all I can think about is last night: the flashing lights behind our car, Carlos frozen, then kissing me, right here. I shiver, even in the heat.

The phone buzzes. Lidia gives me the address, explains that they are waiting for us. Since we're minors, we can't stay for too long. But if we head there, we can regroup. "Go," she says. "Immediately. And call me once you're there."

"Thanks," I breathe.

"And, Rania?"

"Yes?"

"No more lies. Promise?"

I pause. How many lies have the adults told? Everything is a lie! My whole self, not even knowing who my father was. This whole stupid system, where Ammi can't even get a fair hearing. These clapboard houses and fences and beautiful rolling land-scape and miniature golf and fried food—all of it a lie, because it's not for us. But Lidia has never lied.

"I promise," I tell her.

— — —

When I tell Carlos what Lidia said, he sits with his elbows on his knees, subdued. Then he twists off the bed and starts putting his clothes into his backpack. We realize we've bought too much stuff so we drive down Route 6 and buy a big duffel, come back, and jam everything in. We decide to leave after dark because we don't want to attract too much attention. Carlos feels terrible about standing up Marge, so he leaves her a voice message when she's busy at the shop, and says something's come up for next Saturday, but he'll call later.

And everyone at the restaurant? Doris?

We look at each other, guilty. Then I notice my stack of post-cards, sitting by the bed. "We'll leave them a card."

We don't tell Kamal we're leaving, afraid he'll say something to the others at the motel. But we do buy sandwiches and take them to our favorite cove, just as the sun is starting to dip. We sit on our towels while Kamal wades out into the shallows. It's low tide and he keeps going and going. The sun drops, turning the water into ruddy stripes. Streaks of purple and black fill the sky. I'm sure Carlos is going to pull his sketch pad and disappear into his drawing, as he always does.

Instead he puts his arm around my shoulders. His face looks softer, younger somehow. "Thank you," he says.

I can feel the flutter of his heart against mine. "Always," I say.

— — —

Kamal is sleeping when we leave the motel. First the big duffel, then our backpacks. I bought a pillow and blanket for Kamal, which I set up on the rear seats, and then Carlos carries him out to the car. His feet give a little flutter kick, as if he were in the water, as Carlos settles him down. "Where are we going?" he whines.

"A new adventure, mi amor," Carlos whispers.

We slip into the front seat, latch our seat belts. I left the postcard for Doris on our made beds, apologizing. My last lie: *I'm so sorry. My mom had to go into the hospital and she won't be joining us after all. We're going back. Thank you for everything.* I wonder if Doris ever believed my story anyway.

I set my hands on the steering wheel, peer through the windshield. The parking lot is empty. Everyone else is in their rooms or out. I just want to stay in this in-between place, swimming every day. I want to kiss Carlos on the sand. I want to pretend we can do this forever.

Carlos points to my mother's Uber decal. "Thanks for the ride."

"Very funny." I start the car and steer us back onto Route 6, toward the mainland.

On the road. Again. All kinds of words ding inside me. *Fugitive. Illegal. Law breaker.* What about *Kids. Stupid. Running.* The road is a straight humming line, mesmerizing. I imagine the ocean on either side of us, past the darkened mounds of scrub brush and trees. This stretch of land, dissolving into water, a narrow scrap where others once scratched their way to existence, is still here. Why can't we do the same?

Soon we are at the Bourne Bridge and taking 495, looping south of Boston, then west and onward, deeper into Massachusetts. Not many cars, the occasional truck rattling past. Every time a pair of headlights flares into our car, Carlos and I freeze, but after a while we realize it is nothing, another car. We are farther into Massachusetts. I fight against being drowsy. Vermont. We are tunneling into a place where we can stay. For now.

I hope.

I slow to an exit and turn down a narrower road. We go for long stretches before a house rises up, sometimes a barn. The shapes of horses against a fence. I turn to tell Carlos—more for him to draw—but he's resting his head against the window. Asleep. He looks exhausted. Light from the occasional streetlamps slashes across his head and shoulders, a rhythm of dark and light. I think of all he's gone through, how far he's traveled, train, desert, road, subway, here. How long can he keep on before he is too tired to go anymore?

I lean over, touch his bare wrist, where the two fish curl and swim together. A surge of warmth spreads through me. I want to keep him safe.

Gravel spits as we pass through two stone pillars. Carlos sits up, alert. Up ahead, a man waits under a portico. In the wash of headlights, his hair seems to float straight up from his pale head, as if underwater. As we unwind our cramped legs and climb out of the car, he looks both anxious and glad to see us.

"Sam?" I ask.

"Yes." Smiling, he steps forward and takes my hand. Then he turns and grasps Carlos's elbow, as if he needs to hold on. "Shalom. Welcome."

Carlos gives a tight smile, almost as if it is too much to ask for, this welcome.

The building before us looms so large. I go to the back seat and rouse Kamal. "No, Ammi," he murmurs. "Let me sleep!" He tightens his knees against his chest. My heart contracts; sometimes he calls me Ammi. So much is blurred these days.

"I'll take him." Carlos reaches in, heaves up Kamal, and staggers behind us, Kamal's legs dangling against him.

Sam punches a code into a flat gray panel, and a huge door swings open. Before us is an entry with a basket filled with skullcaps, like the ones you see in a mosque. Just beyond, in the hall, cubbyholes and children's drawings tacked to a bulletin board. Around the bend is a huge staircase, with thick carved banisters, and a giant stained-glass window at the landing. The air smells of Lysol and chalk.

Carlos sets down Kamal, who rubs his eyes and looks around him, confused. "Where are we?"

"A synagogue," I tell him. "They've taken us in."

We trudge up past the stained-glass window, around a corner, and climb single file through a narrower set of stairs on the side. I feel like I'm in a story where the children are hidden in secret passages. Once I read about this thing called *sanctuary*—how churches shelter refugees and immigrants. Synagogues too. The idea seemed so fantastic, so unreal.

We gather behind Sam as he jams a key in a door and it swings open to a space smelling of new paint; our feet scuff powder on the floor. He snaps on a light—a bulb hanging from the ceiling. We're standing in a small hall with different rooms branching to the sides.

"I'm so sorry we're not quite finished. We didn't realize it would happen so soon."

"Neither did we," I say.

"Thank you," Carlos adds.

Sam hurries ahead of us, switching on lamps. There's a living room to our right, nicely furnished. A blue sofa, a table with two folding chairs pulled up against a window. Even a TV, unconnected. A bedroom for Carlos with slanted ceilings, a bathroom with a shower stall, smelling of new plastic. A kitchen with a microwave on a cart and a hot plate with two burners. A narrow bedroom with a bunk bed.

Kamal is more awake. "Cool!" he says and patters forward, clambering up to the top bunk. "It's like camp!"

I smile, sad. I wish I could make a game of it.

I sit down on the bottom bunk. Inside me there's a dropping sensation, like an elevator going too fast. It's just all the places we've passed through or fled or lived in, rushing down. I should be relieved—Sam is hurriedly explaining about the keys and locks, while Carlos drags in our duffel bag. But I can't feel that way. Not yet. I swivel around in the room. Magic hands, kind hands, have made all this happen—the newly polished floor, the freshly painted walls. Soon, like Kamal, I will fall into sleep, into dreams, so long, as if we have traveled oceans and continents. And then I see, on the windowsill, someone has left a small plant in a glazed green pot. Leaned against it is a card: *May this home be a sanctuary for those who seek.*

V

Exits North

Chapter Seventeen

The summer grass is turning yellow, leaning back in the sun, and Carlos and I are falling into each other.

Sanctuary. Usually a sanctuary is meant for a family. They were just getting it ready when Lidia called. For us, it means we're not on our own anymore. We're under the watchful and kind eyes of the congregation, people who show up and make sure we're fed and taken care of. A trio of women bring cans and dried goods, cooked meals in Tupperware, lasagna trays. Sam checks on us all the time—sometimes I think he's making an excuse—seeing if a bulb needs changing or fixing a loose hinge on a cupboard. He's an energetic, small man with watery green eyes behind his glasses. He tells me he has a teenage son off visiting his daughter, who's studying in France. He lingers, his big eyes looking over everything. He's probably missing his kids.

Jayne, a lawyer, shows up our first day, sits Carlos down for a long interview, writing heavily on her pad about his case. Lidia calls, and she and Carlos speak for a long time in rapid-fire Spanish. When he hangs up, I ask, "Well?"

He shakes his head. "She isn't sure."

I take his hand. That's all I can do. All he can do. For now.

There are two buildings surrounded by a brick wall—one is the synagogue, a modern structure across the way. The other building must have been some kind of mansion, with dark-paneled walls and a wide carved staircase covered in red carpet. On the first floor is a Hebrew school and currently a small summer camp. The second day a counselor knocks on our door and offers to let Kamal join them. Kamal presses tight against my hip, but I hold his hand, take him down the narrow stairs, and bring him to one of the classrooms. When he sees the counselors are all young, like Carlos and me, he loosens just a bit. His damp fingers still clutch mine as he watches a group of kids build a Lego city in the middle of the room.

"Come join us," a counselor says. She's got reddish hair and gold freckles all over her arms.

He tilts his face to me. "You only have to stay for a little bit, Aapi."

"Just a little bit?"

He gives me a cross look. "I'm not a baby!"

He lets go and heads to a corner, where the Magna-Tiles are. I lean against the wall and watch him flapping and flipping the plastic pieces, concentrating hard as he makes different combinations. Kamal needs something to focus on to make him feel secure. At snack time he joins the others around a table, grinning at the juice box and cookies on a paper plate. A little girl next to him is carefully counting her cookies and when she realizes she has one extra, she gives it to him. He happily crams it into his mouth. I leave, my mood light.

— — —

Carlos and I hold hands and move in and out of the apple trees, up into a maple grove, where the old syrup lines glint like spider threads, strung from trunk to trunk. I take off my favorite jacket, spread it on the dry grass.

We roll toward each other. I can see his stomach, breathing in and out.

Our lips brush. We kiss, pull apart.

"That was nice," I say.

"You're nice." He squeezes my waist.

"No, I'm not. I'm a pain."

"A nice pain." He smiles. "I like it when you get mad. Your eyes get so bright. Like daggers." He cups my hair. "That night at the restaurant, I just wanted us to have a real date."

"But you didn't say that!"

"I could not."

"Why?"

He puts his arm beneath me so the back of my head rests snug against his arm. "I was responsible for you, Rania. For my little hermanito. It wouldn't be right. At home, I would ask permission."

A surge of joy explodes inside me. "I give you permission!" I laugh and kiss him full on the mouth.

— — —

Sanctuary. That word. I want to feel its meaning as these people are offering it: food, camp for Kamal, lawyers. They are trying to smooth away our worrying. But the best part of this time is being with Carlos, every day, exploring the nearby hills.

Over the next week, while Kamal is in camp, Carlos and I

take walks in the sloping woods behind the synagogue grounds. He brings his sketch pad and draws the view as I pull out an old paperback and read, sometimes write in my notebook. I texted Fatima again but she hasn't answered. Maybe that's what we need right now: a little space. Though it hurts.

I'm happy, but also a sadness draws through me, like the shadows lengthening on the ground. Fall coolness seeps through our T-shirts. We kiss some more, then we brush off our legs and climb down the hill. At the synagogue, Carlos teasingly pulls some stray stalks of grass from my hair. At dinner, we're still flushed, so Kamal makes faces at us.

I wish we could tie ourselves, like those syrup lines, to these sturdy people who care for us. On Saturday I wake to the sound of services. I remember, long ago, the call to prayers over scratchy speakers. At the end of the day, Ammi and I would weave through the bazaar, strung bulbs fizzing and spitting in each little stall. During Ramzan, Abu would return in the evening with steaming containers of rice and kebabs. Ammi made a big pot of seviyan kheer and we'd eat that first, gulping down the slippery sweet strands, until she scolded me to save room for the rest.

All these sounds and tastes once locked in the box of the past come spilling out. Nights with my parents. Mild air, bougainvillea on wrought-iron fences. Abu and Ammi's friends sitting on blankets, listening to singers on a stage. They sway, arms around their knees, and sing too. We stay for hours until I fall asleep on Ammi's lap. Then we are in the back of a taxi, streetlamps stripe the windows, the hum and bump of road. *To think this is what those fundamentalists want to bomb away*, Abu remarks. *Hush*, Ammi says, her fingers stroking my hair. *Don't let the driver hear.*

They push their voices low. Another memory: I hear the landline ringing. Ammi slamming it down, in tears. How could I forget so much? Even my old-school uniform—a light blue shalwar kameez, a cardigan for the cold mornings.

As I lean against Carlos, a snatch of ghazal comes to me, and I start to sing, badly:

Tajdaar-e-haram
Tajdaar-e-haram ho nigaah-e-karam
Tajdaar-e-haram ho nigaah-e-karam
Ham ghareebon ke din bhi sanwar jaaenge
Haami-ye be-kasaan kya kahega jahaan
Haami-ye be-kasaan kya kahega jahaan
Aap ke dar se khaali agar jaaenge
Tajdaar-e-haram
Tajdaar-e-haram

"What's that mean?" Carlos asks.

"O king of the holy sanctuary / Bless us with your merciful gaze / O king of the holy sanctuary / So that our days of woe may turn for the better / O patron of the poor, what would the world say / If we return empty-handed from your door? / O king of the holy sanctuary."

I grin at him. "The guy who sings it is *way* cuter than you."

He gives me a teasing push.

Sanctuary. The real meaning: a place where these kind people have returned us to ourselves, to our own memories. Carlos softens against me. We can be kids again, remember who we were before we ran.

We lie on my bed, legs tangled, giggling, recalling old silly stories. I tell him about a party where I grabbed a chicken leg from another girl and she let out a wail so piercing, my mother took me home. He tells me about promenading with his cousin around his town's square, pinching the arm of a girl his cousin liked, so he ruined the whole thing. "We were awful!" I say. We shake with full belly laughs. We kiss, longer. My head fits snug against his throat. He pulls his fingers through my hair. I touch his tattoo, tracing the intertwined fish. Maybe we too are the fish: circling round and round each other.

— — —

"I've got something to show you. Come."

Sam is at our door. He leads us down the road until we arrive at a big barn, with a faded sign hanging from a post: GRETA'S BARN SCHOOL—NO VERY SERIOUS ADULTS ALLOWED, and next to that a wooden table. He unhooks the gate and leads us into the run-down building.

To my surprise, it's a series of brightly painted rooms, some with chalkboards and cubbyholes and hooks. Sam explains that his mother ran a little school here; though he's given most of the items to the synagogue—the chairs and blocks, the sitting cushions and crayons—he can't bring himself to sell the property, not yet. Then he leads us down a narrow corridor to a set of rough wooden pens. Dried and dirty straw lies scattered on the floor.

"Stinky!" Kamal complains.

"This is where the pigs were. And back through that door was the chicken coop. Greta would have the kids gather the eggs and then she'd set them out on the table. People would come by, buy them, and simply tuck the money into a metal box. It was all an honor system."

"Trust," Carlos says.

Sam gives him a sharp look. "Exactly." He grins at Kamal. "You want to see the real barn?"

Kamal jiggles with excitement. "Yes, yes!"

We step outside and then into a huge open space, dusty shafts of light streaming from a giant window. To the left is a platform, thick bales of hay stacked high, and a ladder leading to the loft, spread with more hay.

Sam pauses, head tilted back, taking in the huge space. "My mother survived World War II hiding in a barn in southern France. She always felt that so much of her youth was stolen. And so when she came here—" His eyes look moist. "She wanted to give that back to children."

That's why he volunteers for the sanctuary.

"Kamal, you want to jump in the hay?" He points to the loft.

"Yes!" Kamal squeals. He's afraid, but loves watching brave feats.

Carlos streaks up the slanted ladder while Kamal and I straggle behind, through the itchy, warm hay. We look up to see Carlos, arms out, then he arches his back and sails downward, belly first, landing in the bales with a terrifying thud. My heart jolts into my mouth. Is he okay?

A rustling noise. Carlos emerges from the hay, straw sticking every which way from his hair. He gives a lopsided grin. "¡Qué chido!"

Sam claps his hands. He looks like he wants to cry and laugh. Above, Kamal stands on the edge. "Me too!"

"Kamal, be careful!"

He shoots me an annoyed look.

Carlos has returned to the landing and stands behind Kamal, gently explaining. "Just like in the water, hermanito. Bend your knees. Then jump."

Kamal's legs quiver. He thrusts his arms in front of him, pushes his head down. Then he drops with a squeal, bouncing on the hay bales. "I did it!" he shouts.

We spend the afternoon jumping from the loft. Over and over, laughing each time we sprawl in the crackling straw, then kicking ourselves up again, and dropping, again and again. I feel strangely safe. This is the best kind of sanctuary: not the prayers, that hushed space, where people's devotion makes them care for us. Just three kids, leaping into the air, the hay softly catching us.

— — —

That night, curled again on the sofa with Carlos, a new memory loosens and I describe it to him: I am with Ammi, hurrying to the market. Our flat in Lahore is topsy-turvy from packing. We must buy a new piece of luggage because the zipper was broken on ours. But a man steps out from behind a stall. I do not recognize him; he argues with Ammi. He is handsome, with a strong face, and he takes her pale wrist and pulls on it. I cannot see Ammi's expression—she wears sunglasses all the time from her crying. *You stop that!* I want to say. He reaches for me, holds me clumsily. *Come to Papa,* he says.

You're not my papa! I giggle and try to wriggle away.

He lets go his grip. *You will regret this,* he hisses to Ammi, and then he is gone.

"Whoa," Carlos says. He strokes my back until I grow calm. "That is creepy. How come you didn't remember?"

"I sort of did. In snatches. But that time when we left is such a blur."

"When you run, you run. You don't look back."

I rest against him, shut my eyes. That fear has faded. After a while, he says, "You should tell Lidia. Maybe it will help your mother's case."

"It won't."

"Let her decide that."

He's tracing my knuckles with his thumb. I like to do that to him, as if to understand how his long fingers can do all that drawing. It sends a shivery, tingling sensation through me.

Carlos's scars glow on his neck. I touch them. We are in the dark, which is why he can speak. "Tell me," I say.

His memories rush like a river. It was night. A fence, meant for cows, for animals. The coyote explained that Carlos must go down through the hole beneath the sharp wire. And he did, crawling belly first, and then a sharp pain flared down his neck. Warm liquid soaked his collar. He cried out, but the man smacked him. *Keep going. Pretend it is your jacket that is torn, not you.*

"That was the only way to get across," Carlos tells me. "I had to become a thing."

Now I understand why Carlos holds himself tense, apart, and wary. When he draws, it is a way of saying, *I am not a thing. A headline. I feel. I see.*

I rest my head on his shoulder. There are so many ways to be held. This place with its heavy beams. The barn and its itchy hay. All these kind people, doing what they can. And Carlos, with his own stories, his arms around me, mine around him.

— — —

The door to the living room is shut, but I can hear voices murmuring on the other side. There's a nip in the air—when I climb out of bed, my toes curl on the cold floorboards. Sam and another adult are talking. *School. Registration. Appeal.*

I twist the knob and when the door swings open, I see Carlos sitting on the sofa, Jayne and Sam opposite. Their eyes flash upward at me. "I'm sorry, Rania," Jayne says. "If you don't mind, we need to talk to Carlos alone."

"Is everything okay?"

"Fine, dear. We'll be done soon."

I feel like I've been poked in the chest. I back away and try to busy myself in the kitchen, but all I'm doing is washing the same pot. I check emails. More stuff from Hunter. Freshman orientation. An advisor assigned. A book I need to read. And then an email from Amirah: *Rania, I'm starting to wonder if you want this job . . .* I slam the laptop shut, my eyes stinging. Then I force myself to write back. *So sorry. I had a family emergency. End of August?*

Someone is tapping me on the shoulder. I turn to see Sam. He looks grave. "What's wrong?" I ask.

"Come."

In the living room, Carlos is still staring at the rug. He doesn't even look up when I sit beside him.

"Rania," Jayne says. "My colleagues and I have been going over Carlos's case."

Why did they leave me out?

"The thing is, the situation in the US is very tough."

No kidding.

"He can stay here and we can work on his application. See if we can start the process all over again. But from what I've been seeing, the chances aren't great."

"There has to be something! He told you about the gang—"

"Unfortunately the US doesn't recognize gang threat— especially local ones. His case was always shaky."

"But he can't go back!"

"In three months Carlos will turn eighteen. His chances of being deported as an adult go up exponentially."

A shiver in the back of my neck.

"There is another possibility."

Here my mind is whooshing upward: My mother will adopt Carlos. He'll be part of us. He'll come back to Brooklyn. I have it all worked out.

"Canada," Sam says.

"Canada?"

Now I get why Carlos couldn't look at me. He lifts his head and his eyes are glazed. He's barely holding it together.

"No!" I cry.

Jayne's voice is gentle. "We have some colleagues in Buffalo. Not far from the border. They run a kind of safe house. They can take him in and show him the process so he can start over again. He's allowed under the unaccompanied minors exception. And he says he has a cousin there."

"You barely know him!" I say.

Carlos shrugs. "He's all I've got."

"If someone is willing to claim him, even better. He can make a fresh start."

Claim, I think. Another funny word. Like he's a piece of luggage left at the lost and found.

"No!" I stand up. "That's not right. He can't!"

"Rania," Jayne says mildly. "It's for Carlos to decide."

This stops me. I stare at Carlos. He still has his eyes on the rug. Every bit of me wants to protest. And then I can't stand it. This place feels too tight and close, with its slanted ceiling, its dim light. I rush toward the door, and down the stairs. They call after me, but I don't care. I just keep going—passing the big windows, where I can hear the cheerful sounds of little kids, through the gate and out, onto the road. Past the barn, where I can almost hear our whoops inside, then farther.

How many times can you lose a person? It was hard enough with Abu. Ammi taken away in the night. Then Abu wasn't Abu, so I lost him in another way. And now Carlos.

I've turned into a path and am walking toward a slope where there's a large tree. I throw myself down, blood pumping in my ears, sun blazing on my head. I find some stones on the ground and fling them, again and again. *Run.* That's what Ammi taught me. When it's tough, when you're in trouble, you run. Again and again, we tossed our belongings into suitcases, fooling the man at the airport, then when people said nasty things about Ammi in our apartment house, then the shelter. Ammi signaled: grab the car keys, move, there's always another solution ahead. A place to rest before you push on. But what happens when you don't want to run anymore? When you want the world to stop spinning? To finally stay.

— — —

A crunching noise on grass.

"Hey," Carlos says.

"Hey."

He drops down beside me, dry blades folding around him. "Kamal is almost done with camp. He'll be looking for us."

"Uh-huh."

He nudges me. "Irresponsible sister."

I don't say anything.

"Come on, Rania."

"Come on what? Why don't you try? You can let Lidia and Jayne work on your case! And you can live with us in Brooklyn and—"

He interrupts, "I can't."

"Why not?"

He sighs. I suddenly see that his eyes are circled by bluish shadows. "I watched what my aunt went through. I'm tired, Rania. I'm tired of fighting to be here. You have your mother at least. A job. A lawyer. A family."

"Fight to be with me!"

He bites his lip, lowering his eyes. I hang my head. There's a thickness on my lashes. "Besides, my family is a big mess." I turn to him. "This was our time. On the road. Can't we hold on to that?"

He offers a wavering smile. "We can write. FaceTime. WhatsApp. DM on Instagram."

"I hate social media. I'm bad at keeping in touch. You saw how I messed up with Fatima."

"You suck at being a friend."

"And you just suck."

I can't look at him.

We can't quite leave.

Carlos begins, "My aunt used to tell me this story. About a fisherman who was in love with a woman in her village. He could never find the right words to tell her how he felt. But every night he would go fishing in the night sky of stars. There the words were perfect! Crystal sharp. They said what was in his heart. So he gathered his star-words in his net and set them in a letter by the girl's window. By morning the crystal words had dried to ugly salt flakes. The girl would see nothing but the dirty paper and toss it away. She understood nothing of his love, nothing of what he was saying."

He looks at me. "Don't you see? That's what it's like for me. I was that fisherman who went out to fish in the night sea. I gathered up my words. I was so sure I could move the immigration people. But it didn't work. They can't hear my story."

I start to cry. "I hear your story."

He tightens his fingers around me. "I know, mi amor. I know."

"Mi amor," I repeat. The words blow through me. Mine.

Everything seems to be melting: The sun is tipping lower in the sky, spreading across the ground in a gold glow. The smell of old grass and dirt hovers over us. Carlos slaps his knees, stands, holds out his hand. I take it and we head down the old cow path.

Chapter Eighteen

They agree to let us do it our way. A million instructions. *Text. Call. Check in. See Rachel,* says the woman at the Buffalo place. They install the app that tracks where we are. At first, they wanted to arrange for an escort, but then Carlos begged, "Please, Ms. Jayne, let us have our time." He draped his arm around my shoulders. "I need to say goodbye to my love. Mi amor."

My cheeks flamed, embarrassed that he'd said it in front of everyone!

Jayne's lips twitched into a laugh. "I can't believe I'm letting you do this." She sighed. "I've been there. I remember what it's like to be young." She winked. "And in love."

But they don't know. Not really. They don't know what it's like to be us, kids and not kids. To play in a barn with Kamal and yet sink into the cool shadows of memory. To kiss and hold Carlos, touch his hand, have his drawings pinned to my walls. To want time to go as slow as honey; that we could run and stay in place at the same time. Carlos is the only one in the whole world who gets what it is to be already grown-up and just seventeen at the same time.

It's a straight shot—six hours on a highway—and Jayne has already called ahead to make sure that we can stay there overnight. We're going to a safe house where people get help to file their claim in Canada. Everyone says Carlos's case will be easier than most, so we'll drive there, and then Kamal and I will turn around the next day and come back to the sanctuary. Kamal's strapped into his booster seat, happy because we stopped for snacks before turning onto the highway. At his feet is an insulated bag with sandwiches and bottles of Vitamin Water.

For some reason, the drive has us lighter, sillier, even happier. We're making the most of these hours together, putting off the inevitable. Carlos keeps his arm draped on the back of my seat, occasionally touching my hair. ¡Mi amor! I keep thrilling at the words. No more hiding how we feel. But then I'm laughing too at how corny we are. We sing songs. We play the car license game—we've come up with thirty-two states so far. Carlos makes Kamal do his addition and subtraction tables. Then I grow sad, remembering what we're doing. I dream of a time when we can be together, when I can cross borders easily and throw my arms around Carlos. I try not to pay attention to the pinched knot in my stomach, or the way my hands sometimes tremble on the wheel.

We pull into Buffalo in the afternoon, and stop at a drab-looking brick building surrounded by a huge metal fence, clothing folded over the top edge. Up the concrete stairs, where we are buzzed into an echoey place of noise and commotion. People hurry down corridors, a group of kids sit in a kind of living room with toys and board games. Carlos and I freeze: It's the shelter all over again, only with families dragging their luggage up a set of stairs.

Rachel greets us in a narrow office crammed high with files and papers. She's a heavyset woman, with gold-rimmed glasses that give her face a clear, direct look. Like all the adults, she's kind, but harried. She hands Carlos a clipboard, forms to be filled out. Then she explains that since he's here, she can start the paperwork for asylum in Canada. While he's doing that, so many people stop in—one, a woman who's carrying her baby in a sling on her back. She's crying. "Isn't there anything we can do?" she asks Rachel.

"I'm so sorry. You just have to wait."

There's an air of desperation, of people at a dead end. We're not even the only teenagers on our own—two brothers in Guatemala flag T-shirts slump on a sofa, napping with their arms crossed. Rachel leads us from room to room—crammed offices, a cafeteria and meeting room, the laundry room where people fold their clothes into luggage, a dormitory where people sprawl limp on beds. I tuck my hand into Kamal's as we follow Rachel down a hall to a small room.

She points to a bulletin board pinned with several sheets, and lists of names. "Every day they release the names of the people who can appear at the border crossing."

"How many do they usually release?" Carlos asks.

"Two or three, maybe as much as five."

"Five?" I exclaim, thinking of the rooms and rooms of people here. That woman with the baby is pacing the hall, head tilted, as she presses a cell phone to her ear.

"Since the policy has changed, there's been a surge."

We stare at the names, so many, in their neat rows. I remember what Ammi used to say to me before I left for school: Remember to ask questions, Rania. I wished I asked more of her, all these years.

"And how long could it take?"

Rachel hesitates. "Might be two or three months."

Two or three months. Carlos looks crestfallen. We turn from the lists.

At lunch we're very quiet. I can barely eat—it's a thick pea soup that seems to clump in my stomach—and Carlos just sits, fiddling with his spoon. Rachel was nice enough to give Kamal a little plastic puzzle to occupy him and in between bites, he's trying to get the tiny cars out of their traffic jam.

All good? Jayne texts.

I text a thumbs-up.

Drive back a.m. tomorrow, right?

I send a smiley face.

A guy in a wool hat pulled over his ears and sweatshirt sits down at our table. He has a wide toothy smile and big eyes. "You waiting to get across?"

"Like everyone," Carlos says, and goes back to his soup.

"They tell you two or three months?"

We both nod.

"I'm Keku," he says. "It means Wednesday and that's today."

No kidding. I'm in no mood to make new friends. But we

introduce ourselves and he teases Kamal and then says to us, "There's another way."

We both look up. Keku is a few years older than us—maybe in his twenties. He explains how he's been on the run for years. For a while he sold jewelry and hats on the streets of New York. The cops rarely bothered him about his stand, but he knew he had to get moving again, especially since he was turned down for asylum three times. He heard about this shelter, in Buffalo. Everyone says Canada seems like the only option.

"What's the way?" Carlos asks.

"You can walk across. Not here. But another place."

He pulls out his phone, puts on Google Maps, and zooms in to show us swaths of green and a snaking road. "You just drive to Plattsburgh and then take a taxi. They know where to drop you off. Then you walk across. There are guards there, they arrest you, but you can apply for asylum."

"Is that what you're doing?"

He shrugs. "Miss Rachel says for me it's only a matter of a week or so. I figure if it doesn't happen, I'll do this." He adds, "But don't tell her I showed you this. They don't do it that way here. They say it's not safe."

Grinning, he stands, stretching his arm over his head. "But who knows?"

After he leaves, we fall quiet again but for the *click-click* of Kamal's puzzle. Carlos is fingering his backpack. He hasn't even put his belongings down in the bunk that was assigned to him. I'm calculating, checking Navigator. Six more hours to Plattsburgh.

"What do you think?" I ask.

I can feel his answer.

— — —

Morning mist drifts up from the asphalt yard. The clothes hung over the fence have all been brought in. The corridors are dead quiet. We sneak from our bunks, don't take breakfast. Kamal grumbles, but we managed to fit him into the back seat, still in his pajamas. I figure I've got a few hours before Jayne will notice that I turned off my phone. We're on the highway, headed west.

Rochester.

Syracuse.

Utica.

Then we're plunged into forest, shimmering lakes lined with spears of blue-green spruce. How is it that they can't find room for us? There's so much space here. We're nearing midday and we stop to eat sandwiches at a picnic bench in a rest area.

"Should we check our phones?" Carlos asks.

I stare down at mine. If I turn it on, they can trace where we are. There will be angry messages. We tricked them. Again.

"No."

"You sure?"

I nod.

He doesn't push it. We eat in silence, except to call out the car licenses we see. "Nebraska!" Kamal shouts.

"Wyoming," Carlos points out, as if to top him.

"Whoever gets Alaska wins the prize," I say.

"What's that?" Carlos asks. The only thing I want, the only thing we all want, we can't have. "A Reese's cup," I say. Lame.

Once we reach Plattsburgh, we stop and stretch our legs. It's right on the shimmering expanse of Lake Champlain, and I sense that Kamal, who is staring through the window, is remembering our time on the Cape. So we get ourselves ice cream and then walk for a little while, me and Carlos holding hands, Kamal skipping ahead, as if we're just anyone taking a vacation. We stop at a bench, while Kamal squats at the lake's edge, absorbed in digging a hole with a stick.

"You don't have to be so overprotective of Kamal," Carlos says. "He's stronger than you think."

I nod. "He grew up a lot these last weeks."

Carlos gets up and walks to the water's edge. I join him. He picks up a flat rock and slants it on the water. Only one bounce. I try too, swiveling my wrist, and I get one jump.

"Make a wish," Carlos says. He drops another stone in my palm.

"You first," I tease.

"Nope."

I take a breath, then hurl the stone, not caring if it skips. "That you'll come back for me."

Even as I say it, I know it's impossible. Since he's undocumented and in the system, Carlos won't be allowed into the US for a long time. Am I even staying? Then I think, it doesn't matter. Everything impossible for us and still we did it—we stayed together. As long as we could.

"My turn," he says. He shoots his rock. Two bounces. "You have to keep remembering. To help your mother with your story. For immigration."

"But it's hard!"

"Paciencia."

"Not my strong suit."

"And you have to speak to your family in Pakistan."

"Not fair!" I cry.

He makes a face. "Who said wishes are fair?"

I twist away. "I don't want to ever talk to them."

"Rania, my aunt, she did everything she could. It wasn't her fault." He looks at me, straight on. "Make your family fight for you. For your mother."

Scraps of laughter, parents calling to their kids, scatter around us. The water softens everything, even our sadness. We stretch our arms over our heads. All of a sudden Carlos reaches for me and hugs me, tight. He never does that. I can feel him shaking.

"Thanks," he mumbles, the sound buried in my neck.

"But I didn't do anything! I didn't save you!"

"No. You did something better."

"What?"

"You let me in." He gives me a soft squeeze. "More, it's like you banged on my door and—"

"Pushed my way in," I finish.

"It's just—" He looks away. "I never let someone help me before."

"Me neither," I say softly.

— — —

We turn hushed as we drive the last leg from Plattsburgh. Down a local road, then a left, a right turn. A cluster of vans loom ahead—taxis, I realize—letting people out. All kinds of people—families, dragging their roller luggage; four tall guys with backpacks. They all seem to be headed down a narrow grassy path.

Just beyond, there's a makeshift concrete barrier, where a woman in a uniform stands. Beyond that, some white tents, the kind you see at street fairs.

A confused couple stagger toward us; I can hear snatches of Urdu. The wife's crinkled shalwar sticks between her knees. The husband asks, "This is the border?"

"Yes, right here," I say in Urdu, pointing.

The woman's face breaks open in relief. "Thank you, beta." She starts to pull her luggage but her arms tremble as her luggage bumps into the dirt path. "You are coming?" she asks. I shake my head.

The Canadian border guard is calling to the couple. "Do you have a valid visa?" The couple tell her no. "You do understand if you cross here, you will be arrested?"

The man answers, "But, madam, where else can we go?"

The guard looks like she's been doing this for hours, hearing the same thing. The couple move past her, their luggage twisting and banging on bumpy roots, until they are under the white tent.

Carlos is crouching in front of Kamal. We've told him that Carlos would have to go, without us. Now it hits him. Kamal is blinking, hard.

"Okay, mi amor. I won't see you for a while."

Kamal scrunches his face, tight with a frown. "No!"

"I'm so sorry." Carlos's voice is rough, low. He throws his arm around Kamal, rests his cheek on top of my brother's head, as if breathing him in. I feel as if I'm splitting in two. Carlos is losing so much more. Kamal, me. He turns, and I'm seeing him as I don't want to see him: all alone.

He pulls me, deep, into his arms. I smell and feel all of

him. His fingers loosen my curls. "I always liked your hair," he says with a quiet laugh. "It never stays where it's supposed to be. Like you."

"Very funny," I reply, but my voice is muffled in his collar.

There's just us two, our bodies fierce against each other.

"I better go," he whispers.

When he pulls back, too much air swims between us.

He reaches down for the duffel, hikes his backpack onto his shoulder. He checks his wallet—inside are what's left of his earnings and a little more, from the summer. Then he shifts toward the edge of the road, joining the stream of people who are inching their way to the path. That poor border guard is shouting the same thing all over again—*Do you realize*—Carlos takes his place behind the others. I think about how many times he's done this: become a number, a thing, on a line. He's turning himself hard, protected, to get across.

Be safe, I think.

The line edges forward. Carlos twists around and gives a big wave. Then he turns to the border guard, tells her yes, he completely understands what he's doing, and moves past her. Last I see of Carlos is his beige sketch pad, sticking jauntily out of his backpack.

— — —

In the taxi area, as I'm settling Kamal into his booster seat, one of the drivers says to me, "You wanna make money? There's a ton more waiting at the bus station."

"No thanks."

He flings his cigarette down on the ground. "Your loss." Heaving the door shut, he climbs into the driver's seat and rumbles away.

Kamal asks, "Where are we going?"

I feel him kicking the back of the front seat. But I'm crying so hard it's all I can do to steer the car back down the road, as if through a blurred rainstorm.

"I don't know," I sob.

VI

The Road Back

Chapter Nineteen

Sometimes you think your life story is a straight line, a road humming forward. Maybe Ammi thought her story was a clear way ahead. She went to the best schools. She had a family, fancy clothes, a spot at university. A big wedding and husband.

Me too: I thought Fatima and I were the same.

I thought my biggest problem was Ammi trying to be me.

I thought I got my height from Abu.

I was so focused on what was ahead, that I didn't understand what was behind me. It was too complicated. It didn't make a clean story.

What good is a story if you don't know all the parts?

— — —

Since we got back from the Canadian border three days ago, I sleep in Carlos's bed. Sam and the others were pissed at what we did, but then they leave me alone. The pillow still smells of Carlos: of his soap, his hair, the chalky powder of pastels. When I shut my eyes, all I see are highway lanes, thrumming motion. Then sleep. And dark. I take Kamal downstairs to camp, a few hours later bring him up, and heat up one of the dinners the volunteers leave for us. I let him watch videos or TV. I don't walk the grounds or take Kamal to the barn to jump onto the hay bales. I keep my phone off. The Canadian authorities probably took Carlos's phone and it will be a while before I hear from him. Even so, it will probably be through the lawyers. I don't look at my emails, the orientation announcement, the book list. I haven't written to Amirah. What's the point? I can't go forward or back. I scribble in my notebook, try to write.

> *Disappeared.*
> *The word I learned when Abu didn't come back.*
> *When a boy I loved hiked his backpack*
> *Crossed a border, gone.*
> *The gunky space under sink pipes.*
> *Dusty floor-bottom where I dropped my barrette.*
> *The place where things go to die.*
> *Abu also taught me you can put an "un" before a word*
> *Make it the opposite.*
> *Why can't that be true of a person?*
> *Why can't I put an "un" before his memory*
> *Restore him*
> *To me.*

— — —

A happy, flushed Kamal jumps onto my bed holding two dripping ice cream cups.

"Don't spill!" I push aside my notebook.

I thought Kamal would fold into sadness when Carlos left, but he walks around the sanctuary apartment with a puffed-out chest, declaring that he can take his own showers or pour his own cereal. He leaves the cup on the night table and dashes off. Slowly, I start spooning the ice cream, which soothes.

I feel a wave of nausea. A sour taste on my tongue. I set the cup down. A new memory lets loose in me, in a long hot strand: Hakim, the chowkidar. Ammi upstairs resting in the dark. She does that a lot since Abu disappeared. A tall man takes my hand. His aviator glasses shine so I can't see his eyes. I am in the back seat of a car; the man is driving, promising me ice cream. There's another man next to me. He tells me, "Lie on the floor. Make yourself round like an ice cream scoop." He laughs like it's a joke. I do not think it is funny but I do as I'm told. The floor smells of rubber and gasoline. The man's shoes are turned up, showing mud. I can feel the road thrumming beneath, the twisting and turning. I want to throw up.

The man with the muddy shoes says, "What's the plan, yaar?" Silence from the front.

The car stops. My legs hurt when I unwind to the pavement. An ice cream cup is pushed into my hand. Strawberry scoop. I don't like strawberry! I blink. How did we come back to our building? Inside the gate, Hakim is gone. We are standing next to Abu's scooter, which has sat there since he went away. A silver flash in one man's hand. The scooter bumps down. "You tell your mother if she asks too many questions, next time, you won't come back," the tall man says. He knocks the ice cream out of my hand. Pink foam-splatter on concrete. I cry. "Get out of here!" Legs pumping up the stairs, so hard, my knees burn.

When I see Ammi with her dark worried eyes, my mouth clamps shut. Because she told me. *Don't tell anyone. Don't speak of troubles.* And my nani said to me: *Your ammi, always making so much trouble.*

I drop the scene like an ugly snake into a memory hole.

Now, in Carlos's room, the ice cream on the sill is a sticky pink soup. I pull out my notebook, write down, fast, what I recall until my wrist and fingers ache and there's nothing left. Then I dive into sleep.

— — —

The phone vibrates, nearly jumping off the top of the dresser. I push my face deeper into the sweaty pillow. The call can't be from Carlos because they've taken his phone away. I roll over. A buzzing noise.

I snatch up the phone.

"Rania!"

I bolt upright. "Ammi?"

"I'm back! In Brooklyn! Lidia got the release. I told you she works miracles!"

"Miracles," I say dully.

"That's great." I rub my temples. Why did Ammi get released? Why is Carlos gone? Why can't the world stop spinning?

"We had a bond hearing. The judge said I wasn't a flight risk or a threat to the community and I have a right to await our appeal." She adds, "I'm sure it's because I have one child who is a citizen, another who is such a good girl, an honor student!"

"Ammi, the judge doesn't care about things like that. Did he say that?"

"No, but it's what he believes!"

"Whatever."

"Now, I am very cross with you, Rania. I heard what you did."

She chatters on until I break through. "Ammi—"

"You had Lidia at her wit's end. And you lied—"

"Listen to me!" I shout.

She stops.

"I know," I say. "I know about my father."

Quiet on the other end. Then a small sound. Is she crying? I've rarely heard Ammi cry.

"Come home," she whispers. "Just come home."

— — —

Sam and the sanctuary team stand in a circle in the gravel drive; one by one, they hug us, ruffle Kamal's hair. They've given us a Styrofoam cooler with food and drinks, a puzzle for Kamal. I feel as if I'm saying goodbye to all that's happened— the shelter, the motels, the Cape, the apartment on top of a synagogue, to who I became this summer.

"Straight through, Rania," Sam says. "Promise?"

"I promise." I hug him, hard. "Thank you so much."

This time I will obey. I have no choice. Because I am one of the lucky ones: I can set my hands on the steering wheel and return to my mother. But there are still others crying at night. That old couple bumping their luggage on the dirt trail to the border. Boys like Carlos stepping toward a border, hoping for the best.

I turn on the ignition, turn back toward home.

— — —

She is smaller than I remember. She stands in the apartment doorway, her shoulders hunched, and tips up on her toes to hug me.

"Ammi!" Kamal shrieks. He flings his arms around her neck and sobs.

"It's okay, my little boy," she whispers. "It's okay."

We talk and we cry as Ammi and Kamal cling to each other. Ammi and I glare at Mrs. Flannery through the back window. We let Kamal bounce on his bed and then he stretches on his stomach on the floor, absorbed with play. Then we go from room to room, marveling. The apartment is almost the same, even the plastic containers left upside down to dry on the rack. We return to sit on the edge of my bed. It's quiet; just the clicking sound of Legos.

"He's grown." Ammi slides her arm around my waist. "You too. You did a good job, Rania."

I don't answer, angry questions sparking through my veins.

"You want to see what Carlos gave me?" Kamal asks.

"Carlos?" Ammi asks.

"Our friend," he says. "He came with us. He was so cool!"

"To Uncle's?"

"Everywhere! We lived in a motel. And we saw whales!"

"And you swam a lot," I remind him. "You even jumped off a dock."

Ammi turns, crosses her arms across her chest. "You have a lot to explain," she says sternly.

So do you.

— — —

After we eat takeout and Kamal goes into the bath, Ammi and I sit down together. When she tried to help Kamal, he told her firmly, "No, Ammi, I can do it on my own!" She watched, amazed, as he shut the bathroom door, later unfolded his pajamas from our luggage, and slid under the covers. "Don't hold me," he told her. "I'm a big boy."

Ammi is different too. No rushing to the next task—laundry, cooking, poring over her real estate books. She sits in the living room, feet curled beneath her. In the dim light I see more lines etched around her eyes, her mouth. There's a small wobble in her head.

"Why didn't you tell me about my real father?" I finally ask.

She stares down at her hands, shorn of the rings she likes to wear, making her look even smaller. Everything about her seems stripped down, which makes me less afraid of her. "I could not stay, Rania. He was not a good man."

"What do you mean?"

"He was petty. Small-minded. Controlling. His family too. They told him to get control of his wife, that I was shaming them. I was dying. Don't you see? I was never meant for that world. I didn't fit." She gives me a weak smile. "Can you imagine? I drive an Uber! Everything about me was wrong. The way I think. The way I speak. Only your abu—"

"He's not my abu."

"Yes, he is." She adds softly, "He was."

"But why did you keep it from me?"

She hangs her head. "I needed to handle it, Rania. I always handle things. You know that."

She wraps her hands around mine. "After Naved's disappearance, I received terrible phone calls warning me not to investigate. One night I was so afraid, I called Salim Uncle. I thought I could trust him. But he betrayed me. He told Fawad." A chill slices through me.

"I had to flee with you. Your father already thought my life was risky. Once he knew of Naved's disappearance, of the threats, I would have had no power. They would say I was not a responsible mother. That you didn't belong with me. He began to harass me. Calling at all hours. Stalking. He had everything on his side. Money. Lawyers. Even my own family, who believed I'd made a mess of things. He would have taken you away from me. He always said I was reckless." She sighs. "And maybe I was."

My lids burn, hot with grit. I was so ready to be angry, but this is the most honest my mother has ever been. She left because of me. To keep me.

"Am I in danger?"

"Since we settled here, he did not fight me. But he used his influence." Her eyes are full, shiny. "Even with Salim, my own brother. That's why we never saw your uncle when he moved here. Fawad poisoned how they saw me. A bad mother."

"Uncle said you came to him for help here. But he couldn't do it."

"Is that what he told you?"

I nod.

"Ah, these men, with their pride! Fawad had loaned my brother money at home, for a business. Poor Salim, nothing ever quite works out for him. That's why he emigrated—because his business went bust. And he was indebted to Fawad."

"And now? What happens to us?"

"Now—if I am deported back, if *we* are—Fawad will get you. Of that I'm sure. My life with you will be over."

"But I'm almost eighteen. A grown-up."

She sighs. "He has his ways. He will make everything very hard for me. For you."

I swallow. "Kamal?"

"He will stay with me. He is Naved's."

"But we're a family!"

She smiles tiredly, and puts her hand on the side of my face. "Yes, we are. Always."

That night, I lie in my old bed, clenched against my mother's whole story. Now I understand: her iron pride, her secrecy. Maybe when she went for her interview, the judge sensed it was not the whole truth. She would not beg. She would not fit into a neat box. I roll over, punch the pillow, and try to get some sleep.

— — —

Early hour: the sky looks like streaks of milk. I slip from bed, flip open my laptop, and send the emails I've been avoiding. Then I sneak out of the apartment, buy a café con leche, cradling the cup as I sprint up the concrete stairs to the park. An old man is doing tai chi, his arms moving like a waving octopus. Another man, shirtless, is walking backward. A little dog sniffs at my feet until he's yanked by his owner and trots away. Otherwise the park lies still.

From my pocket I pull out a phone card. I put in the number from the scrap of paper I've been carrying with me. The bleating of an overseas call—then it is picked up. "Hallo?"

"Hello, Uncle. It's me, Rania."

"Rania! What a surprise! How are you, sweetie?"

"I'm good. Ammi's back."

"Oh, I am glad."

We chat about my cousins, about him living with his in-laws, and then our talk dwindles, awkward. Finally I ask, "Uncle, when Ammi decided to come here, what happened with my father?"

He sighs. "It was not good. The prospect of you leaving set him off. Fawad has a temper. Sad to say, I think he was glad of what happened to Naved. He could use it in some way."

My head spins. I watch the man walking backward on the path. That's what I'm doing—walking backward into something old and terrible. I press the heel of my palm against my burning eyes. I don't want to hear this. I say, "My mother has to get asylum. That's the most important thing."

"Asylum! What does she need that for? That's for poor people."

You have no idea, I think.

"Come, come, Rania. Why should you suffer? Come back to Pakistan. It will be so good. You will see your cousins! You'll be where you belong. With family."

I try to brace myself against him, the affection in his voice. "Ammi—"

"Your mother made her choice years ago." He is cold. "It doesn't have to be yours."

Quiet stretches between us. His words sink into me. Is he right? I could go back. Or maybe we should slip over the border, just like Carlos. Why make everything so hard? I remember what Carlos said: *Make your family fight for your mother. For you.* I say, "Uncle, you have to help us. Help Ammi."

"Didn't I do that before? Signing that paper—"

"This is different." Then I explain that he should make a statement for our appeal, about all he knew of her situation, the phone calls, Fawad's threats, before we left.

"I need you to be her bhayia." I say *brother* in Urdu, not English, drawing the sound out. As if to throw him a line, across the oceans and continents, back to us.

— — —

Even from far away I can see Fatima: walking down the path with two cups of coffee, her flip-flops snapping at her heels. I'm calmer. After the call, I walked around and around the park until my body stopped humming.

We hug, tight. "Fa-Fa," I say.

"Ra-Ra."

We breathe into each other.

"I brought you a coffee," Fatima says, as she pulls away. "But you've already got one."

"Mine's cold." I take the cup from her and pop open the top. "Thanks."

Fatima sits down, and for the first time I see the milky tint to her skin, her arms like pale brown silk. Why didn't I notice this before? She's got blue eye shadow on her lids and thick eyeliner. Her hair has been brushed and sprayed into stiff ringlets. "What's with the whole do?" I ask.

She tips her head down. "I went out. With a boy my parents picked."

I make a face. "You're kidding."

"What, you don't approve?"

"No, Fatima! It's not that."

Finally, she says, "Look, it's just easier. If I do it, I can go to college this year."

"I get it."

"Do you?"

"No," I admit. My best friend seems a stranger to me—obeying her parents, going out with a boy they picked for her. Looking like an older woman on a cheesy movie poster.

"It was hard. You were gone. You got to be on the road! Free!"

I snort. "Free? Your family left me cold. I had no one. I only had Carlos to help me figure it out." Tears start to leak out of my eyes. I hate her seeing me like this. I'm the strong one in our pair. The sensible one.

"Oh, Ra-Ra—"

She reaches for me, but I hunch away, sip my coffee. Then I sneak a look. Fatima is staring at her feet.

"So what was it like?" I venture.

"What?"

"The date."

She sighs. "It was actually pretty boring. He doesn't even know who the Beats were."

"Most people don't. They're just some boring white dudes."

She swerves to face me, her hazel eyes lit up. "Look, one day there's gonna be some guy they pick who I like. I've made my peace with that, Rania. You . . . you can't judge me. I can't have my best friend judging me all the time."

"Is that how you feel?"

She tilts her head so a curl loosens over her cheek and I can't see her expression. "Yes. That's exactly how it feels."

"I'm sorry."

We both stare at the jagged outline of Manhattan in the distance. There was a time when the two of us looked at this view and felt ourselves going in the same direction. But I set my hands on a steering wheel and went on the road. I kissed a boy, I found out who my father was, what danger we lived with. And Fatima went on to find something else, about herself. If I learned anything this summer, I claimed what was mine. Maybe Fatima and I both did, in our own ways.

She looks at me slyly. "I did tell my father he may be able to pick out a husband, but he can't pick my BFF. In fact, he better lay off her."

"You said that?"

Her eyes are shining. "You bet."

The harbor shimmers in late-summer sun. I fish out the small bag of tiny ridged white shells and drop it in her palm. "Freedom," she whispers.

"It's overrated," I say, and laugh.

"Is it?" Her eyes are pleading. She wants me to forgive her but for what? She didn't do anything wrong. She tried to help. So why am I still so sore at her? For being different from me? For having a family that holds her too tight and loves her? How can I ever explain all I have been through, all I've come to know? And then she sets down the bag, and reaches for my hand. Her skin is not fragile, but warm, firm.

"Tell me," she says. "Tell me everything."

— — —

Lidia opens her door, gives me a hard look. It's Labor Day, but she's made a point of meeting us here at the office. "Where I grew up, they'd bring out a switch, Rania. Running off like that! You should have heard those shelter folks up in my face all the time."

"We've talked about it," Ammi says. "Rania says she's sorry."

"I do?"

"Rania!" The old Ammi is back.

I bow my head. "I'm sorry," I mumble. I look at Lidia. "Truly. I didn't mean to scare everyone."

"All right then. Come into my office."

Ammi and Kamal stay in the waiting room while I sit across from Lidia. First I unfold a piece of paper and pass it to her. "This is roughly what Salim Uncle told me. He promises he will send a statement that's notarized."

She folds the paper and sets it to the side. Her chair squeaks as she rolls closer to me. "Okay. On to you."

I give her my notebook, where I wrote down my memories, best I could remember. Her brow bunches as she reads. She sets it down and pumps me with more questions, so many questions. I tell her about the time I came into the bedroom and Abu was

228

lying in the dark, his head bandaged. The calls in the middle of the night, Ammi slamming the receiver down. The men who took me for ice cream.

"So you lived with danger even after your father disappeared?"

I shut my eyes. The Wellfleet pond rushes up: a space of green surrounding me. My own breaths, the slashing motion of my arms. That word—*danger*—glimmers up from the murky pond bottom, like a knife. There it was, all along. I clutch it, hard.

"Yes," I say firmly. "We lived with a lot of danger."

"You were scared?"

Another word, locked away. A little sob escapes. "All the time."

When I blink my eyes open, I'm drained and sweaty. I've been grasping Lidia's wrist, leaving tiny indentations. I yank away.

Lidia is very still. "You did good, Rania."

"Will it make a difference?"

"I'm not certain. We're back to waiting on the appeal. But we can file your statement and Salim's, as a supplement. Once in a blue moon they actually send an application back to the original judge for reconsideration." She taps her pen on the pad. "You've given us more context. The peril both you and your mother were in. Your biological father. We may want to rethink the terms by which we're applying. It might be easier in some ways. Sometimes domestic violence . . . well, it plays into a certain—"

"Story," I supply.

"Yes."

We sit facing each other, suddenly awkward.

"You know, it was Carlos who told me to do this. Tell you about my memories. He thought it could help."

She smiles. "Smart boy."

Tears well in my eyes and I blink them back. "He is."

She gets up, touches my shoulder. "My colleagues heard from Carlos."

I jump up, my heart leaping into my throat. "Is he okay?"

"He's fine. He's in a shelter right now."

"Oh no!"

"He'll be okay, Rania."

"Can I talk to him, please?"

She clasps both my hands. "He told me to tell you—be patient."

I blink back tears, bite my lip, and nod. I will try. But it won't be easy.

Gently, Lidia nudges me into the waiting room, where Ammi glances up at me, her eyes flashing with worry. Then she clicks off the light and says to my mother, "Go, Sadia. Enjoy the holiday with your family."

— — —

When we step outside, thick late-summer heat eddies around us. All the offices are shut down, the streets quiet, but for an occasional cab or a delivery boy pedaling his bike.

"So hot!" Ammi declares. "The subway will be a bloody furnace. That's one thing I didn't miss."

"What did you miss?" I ask.

She is surprised. "Why, you both, of course."

For some reason, I don't believe her. Maybe it's because I'm just learning who my mother is, who I am. I keep glancing at her, waiting for some new secret to spring out.

"Have you registered for all your classes?"

"Yes," I say.

"Which ones?" I tell her: a class on Victorian literature, since I placed out of freshman comp, then math, intro bio, an anthropology course.

"Victorian was my favorite," she murmurs.

"I know."

"When I did my MPhil, I wrote on *Mill on the Floss*. Not considered Eliot's best, but I loved it. How apt! A brother who forsakes his sister."

She's told me this a million times. But I realize she's giving me a clue about her, her past. She's speaking to all those people who would not hear her. That's why she repeats herself. To tell me her story, in her own way.

Before we cross the little park near City Hall leading to the subway, I pause. Kamal picks up a stick that he runs, clattering, across the metal fence.

"Ammi," I start.

She looks at me.

"What if your appeal doesn't work?"

"It will work."

"Ammi. Don't lie."

She swivels. "I don't know, Rania! Maybe I will try Canada, like your friend. I can't go back. This is all I have. You, Kamal, are all I have. There I am only Naved's widow. The wife of Fawad who did him wrong. Here I can be anyone."

"You're an Uber driver!"

She lifts her chin. "And what of it? That is nothing to be ashamed of."

She's right—and the shame burns right through me. We both shift uneasily on the bench.

"About this Carlos boy," my mother begins.

I flush.

"They kissed!" Kamal chimes.

I turn and give him a little kick.

"What was it about him that you liked?" Ammi asks.

I want to say: watching him draw, the tiny jump in my chest when he'd return from working the morning shift, smelling of cooking oil. The dare, the exhilaration every time we came up with a new plan on the road. It was the feeling that I was protected and also, I was protecting him. And most of all he taught me patience. Paciencia. How to listen to myself.

Instead I say, "He was awesome, Ammi. He could draw anything! Anyone! Everyone loved Carlos. Kamal adored him. And most of all, he wasn't afraid." I pause. "He taught me to . . . wait."

Ammi smiles broadly, puts her palms on either side of my head, and says, "You are my daughter then."

A sob clutches my throat. "But I lost him, Ammi. How am I ever going to live with that?"

Her face crumples. "Oh, my child." She puts her arms tight around my neck. We sway, shoulders pressed, her sandalwood scent and hair mingled with mine. I picture Carlos in a shelter, by himself, and I remember a line my mother sang: *I should be patient, you say, without my love.*

Then I pull away, wiping my eyes. "Please, no more lies. At least not to me, ever."

She hesitates. She's hidden her past for so long. But finally it has been flung open. "Okay-okay."

She gets up, slaps her thighs. "Chalo. We go home, yes?"

I don't get up from the bench. It's as if I'm wedded to its slats. "Ammi, I'm not going back with you." Seeing the cloud of hurt on her face, I add quickly, "I want to walk back. By myself." I add brightly, "I got a job working in a bookstore."

"Which one? Is it the one in Park Slope? I always go there—"

I hold my hand up. "Ammi, it's my job. Not yours."

She offers a crooked grin. "Okay-okay."

We stand. We're on the pavement that curves toward the entrance to the Brooklyn Bridge. A few bicyclists swerve down the bridge ramp. It seems that everyone has left the city: All the people with cars and houses, with money, have left or are shut into their air-conditioned apartments.

"Makes me think of Whitman," Ammi murmurs. "'Crossing Brooklyn Ferry.'"

Smiling, I quote: "'Others will enter the gates of the ferry and cross from shore to shore.'"

Ammi answers, "'Others will watch the run of the flood-tide.'"

We both laugh. Our hands find each other's. "I still believe that, Rania. There is room for us, in this country."

I feel her fingers, twisted light in mine. How much we share— books, words, poetry. Snatches of memory, the good ones too. Our life with Abu. But Ammi wanted me to finish out her story. I can't do that. Maybe that's what Carlos and this whole strange summer gave me. How to stay still and find my story. My words. Like the fisherman in Carlos's tale, maybe mine won't be heard either. But at least I tried. At least I set them down, gave them to Lidia.

"Ammi!" It's Kamal stamping his feet. "It's ho-ot! I don't want to take the subway!"

Ammi wipes her wet face. "Come, come, you lazy boy. I have a secret for you. There's pizza after we get out of the subway in Brooklyn. Will that help?"

He grins widely. "Yes!"

She lets me go, takes Kamal's hand, and walks toward the subway stop. I pause to watch her: tiny, stubborn woman. Even Kamal is determined as he marches ahead. Then I cross over to the long path that leads to the bridge.

At the midway point, where the bridge widens, I stop, watching the ferryboats plow the river. It's so hot even my wrists are sweating. Heat shimmers off the wooden slats. The suspension lines glint. All of this—the bicyclists whizzing down the narrow path, the water stabbed with diamonds of light, the jammed buildings, and the continent that now I know lies beyond, stretching to marsh and land and ocean—all of it mine too.

By the time I reach the other side, my shirt is damp and crumpled. I head over to Flatbush Avenue, thread through narrow streets, and come to a stop before the bookstore. Cupping my palms on the glass, I peer inside. Even though it's a holiday, there is Amirah at the front counter, wearing a beautiful red headscarf, nodding at a customer. I step inside, wave. She waves back. The door swings shut behind me.

"I'm here," I say.

AUTHOR'S NOTE

Just as my characters went on a road trip, I too took a journey for this novel. Along the way I was helped by many people offering guideposts and insight into the complicated, fragile landscape of immigration and asylum law. While I have done my best to honor the reality of immigration policies, this is a work of fiction that aims to get at the essence of an imagined story.

This story originated one day when I was riding a subway in Brooklyn and a vision of Rania appeared right before me: black hair, black combat boots, a ferocious teenage poet wanting to gulp in the city. Soon after, I was standing under the slanted ceilings of Bnai Keshet in Montclair, observing congregants figure out how to make the space into a sanctuary.

That summer, I left for a residency at VCCA Moulin a Nèf, in Auvillar, France, where, the very first night, I stumbled upon an albergues—a welcoming hostel for pilgrims who walk the Camino de Santiago.

This book was born out of that spirit of pilgrimage and sanctuary, marking the third novel I have written exploring the post-9/11 experience for immigrant and especially Muslim teenagers. When Rania stands before the Brooklyn Bridge, she invokes the spirit of Walt Whitman, who keenly understood the transformative possibilities of America, which has always been changed and replenished by each new, surging wave of people.

Two significant backdrops also inform this story: the draconian immigration policies instituted in the US in 2018, when asylum-seeking families were separated at the border, and the ICE crackdowns and dragnet sweeps that became a regular, terrifying occurrence for immigrants. The other backdrop is the increasing authoritarianism, suppression, and censorship of journalists in many countries. At the time of Abu's "disappearance," violence and murder of journalists in Pakistan was at an all-time high. Today, throughout the world, journalists are imperiled for doing their job by reporting the truth. It is to them I—and all of us—are forever indebted.

ACKNOWLEDGMENTS

A huge shout out to Lauren Blodgett, inspiring founder of The Brave House, an organization for immigrant young women and gender-expansive youth. She allowed me to be a fly on the wall with her in immigration court, and graciously vetted this manuscript. So too did Loretta Lopez and Afia Nathaniel, who combed the manuscript for cultural nuances. Stephanie Gibbs of Safe Passage, Dan Kesselbrenner—former executive director of the National Immigration Project—and Andrew Painter provided further legal clarification.

Many people encouraged and inspired me as I wrote: Rabbi Elliot of Bnai Keshet in Montclair gave of his time, explaining the sanctuary movement, and he led me to Charlene Walker of Faith in New Jersey. My fellow organizers from the Montclair Writers Group created a reading of immigrant literature, called "Borders of the Heart," to raise money for families stranded at the border.

As I write these acknowledgments, I am ending one journey to begin a new one: I decided to leave my position as a professor at William Paterson University to write full-time. It is a bittersweet moment: my students have always helped me "keep it real," and my colleagues have provided a kind and supportive environment.

Wendy Lamb and Dana Carey pushed me to bring clarity and precision to this story. Sharyn November gave a crucial read at a key time. Gail Hochman is always there, cheering for me. Dorothy Kelly helps keep my work life humming. My husband, Marc, is my constant companion in this sojourn of marriage and creativity. Both my boys, Sasha and Rafi, gave me insight into teenage speech. The friendship of Bonnie Friedman, and of our fellow writer-readers in the Grove Street Group, kept me running creatively even when my fuel gauge was empty. And a National Endowment for the Arts Fellowship in Fiction gave me more space for all my writing.

Wellfleet—that windswept bit of land at the edge of the continent—has provided sustenance, inspiration, and family rejuvenation for years.

Thank you all.

For more information:
Committee to Protect Journalists: cpj.org
National Immigration Project: nationalimmigrationproject.org

GHAZALS/SONGS

MIRZA GHALIB

Let's Live in That Place / Rahiye ab aisi jagah

Let's live in that place where there's no one, let's go,
Where no one knows our tongue, there's no one to speak to.
We'd build a house without doors and walls,
Have no neighbours, watchmen forego.
In sickness no one to nurse us, enquire,
If we died, no one to mourn us, no!

rahiye ab aisī jagah chal kar jahāñ koī na ho
ham-sukhan koī na ho aur ham-zabāñ koī na ho
be-dar-o-dīvār sā ik ghar banāyā chāhiye
koī ham-sāya na ho aur pāsbāñ koī na ho
padiye gar bīmār to koī na ho tīmārdār
aur agar mar jāiye to nauha-khvāñ koī na ho

MIRZA MUHAMMAD HAKIM

Partial lyrics for O King of the Holy Sanctuary / Tajdar-e Haram:

O king of the holy sanctuary
Bless us with your merciful gaze o king of the holy sanctuary
So that our days of woe may turn for the better
O patron of the poor, what would the world say
If we return empty-handed from your door?
O king of the holy sanctuary

Tajdaar-e-haram
Tajdaar-e-haram ho nigaah-e-karam
Tajdaar-e-haram ho nigaah-e-karam
Ham ghareebon ke din bhi sanwar jaaenge
Haami-ye be-kasaan kya kahega jahaan
Haami-ye be-kasaan kya kahega jahaan
Aap ke dar se khaali agar jaaenge
Tajdaar-e-haram
Tajdaar-e-haram

Permission granted by Zahra Sabri, translator, from "Tajdaar-e-Haram" lyrics song sung by Atif Aslam for Coke Studio Pakistan, a tribute to Sabri Brothers.

MOHAMMED QULI QUTUB SHAH

1

I can't ever drink my drink without my love
I can't ever breathe; I sink without my love
I should be patient, you say, without my love
How unfair! I can't even blink without my love . . .

Piyaa baaj pyaala piyaa jaaye naa
Piyaa baaj jek til jiyaa jaaye naa

Kaheethey piyaa bin saboori karoon
Kahhiya jaaye amma kiyaa jaaye naa

Reproduced in arrangement with HarperCollins Publishers India Private Limited from the book *Hazaron Khawaishen Aisi: The Wonderful World of Urdu Ghazals* selected, edited, and translated by Anisur Rahman.

ABOUT THE AUTHOR

MARINA BUDHOS is the author of award-winning fiction and nonfiction. Her novels for young people are *The Long Ride, Watched, Tell Us We're Home,* and *Ask Me No Questions.* Her nonfiction books are *Remix: Conversations with Immigrant Teenagers* and two coauthored books, *Eyes of the World: Robert Capa, Gerda Taro & The Invention of Modern Photojournalism,* and *Sugar Changed the World,* written with her husband, Marc Aronson. Budhos has received an NEA Fellowship in Fiction, has been a Fulbright Scholar to India, and was a professor of English at William Paterson University.

marinabudhos.com